Feels Like Home

an Oyster Bay novel

Olivia Miles

~ Rosewood Press ~

Also by Olivia Miles

The Misty Point Series
One Week to the Wedding
The Winter Wedding Plan

Sweeter in the City Series
Sweeter in the Summer
Sweeter Than Sunshine
No Sweeter Love
One Sweet Christmas

The Briar Creek Series
Mistletoe on Main Street
A Match Made on Main Street
Hope Springs on Main Street
Love Blooms on Main Street
Christmas Comes to Main Street

Harlequin Special Edition
'Twas the Week Before Christmas
Recipe for Romance

ISBN 978- 0999528402

FEELS LIKE HOME

First Edition: November 2017

Feels Like Home

an Oyster Bay novel

Chapter One

It took eleven minutes to pack three suitcases. Two hours to make it over the state line. Half the night to stop the tears from flowing. And an instant to undo a ten-year marriage.

Ten years. It felt like a hundred years and ten seconds all at once. Ten years since that sweltering July day when Margo Harper had walked down the rose-scattered aisle of St. Mary's Church of Charleston, clinging tightly to her father's arm, her lace wedding gown trailing behind her thanks to the impressive six-foot train, trying not to faint from the combination of nerves and heat, and joined hands with Ashley Lynn Reynolds.

That's right. She had married a man named Ashley. Ashley *Lynn*.

There was a reasonable explanation, of course. His

mother was a diehard fan of *Gone with the Wind*, she announced in that first meeting, as she poured two glasses of homemade lemonade from a sweating pitcher and handed one to Margo. They were seated on the back porch of the family home, just the two of them, side by side in rock hard wicker chairs in a supposed effort to get to know each other, though it seemed that Nadine was more interested in sizing up her future daughter-in-law than bonding over the untouched strawberry shortcake. When the announcement had been made, a mere five minutes into arriving at the old, plantation-style house that had been in the Reynolds' family for generations, Nadine's face had gone a ghastly shade of white, and she had excused herself for an unnerving amount of time before returning to her guests with a sugary smile, and the offer of having some alone time with Margo. *Gone with the Wind* was her favorite movie, she'd said, eyeing Margo carefully. She'd watched it one hundred eighteen times to date. If she'd ever had a girl, she would have named her Tara. As she was given just one child, a son, Ashley was it.

Margo had managed a polite smile, tilted her head, tried to stop her heart from pounding at the way Nadine's icy blue eyes didn't quite catch her smile. She might have even given a little "Ah!", as if the mystery was finally solved, as if any woman's love for a historical film could justify naming a baby boy Ashley in the early 80's. Margo sipped the lemonade, blinked at the tartness, and then, perhaps from the onset of heat stroke or maybe just a poor attempt to make conversation, inquired, "Why not Rhett?"

It was the obvious choice, after all. Rhett was the leading man. The alpha male. Rhett was a strong, masculine, swoon-worthy type of name, whereas Ashley... Well, you didn't see that name on many blue toddler cups, now did you? You did, however, see it on the personalized princess crowns that her niece Emma liked to wear. Not that Margo ever pointed this out, tempting as it was at times over the years, especially when Nadine got a little too vocal about her wish for future grandchildren and her hope that the first-born son would be named after her father. Lindsay. (Lynn had been a nod to Lindsay, but Ashley Lindsay didn't have the right ring to it, Nadine said.)

It was clear from the pinch between Nadine's brow, and the silence that followed, that Margo had made a misstep in that first meeting. Margo opened her mouth, desperate to backpedal, but the truth was that she'd always been a terrible liar. Terrible. She'd get all red in the face and lose eye contact, or hold it for too long, sometimes without blinking, and then she never did know when to finally look away...naturally. Or she'd go overboard. Say things that could never be true, that no one would buy, like the one she told to her then future mother-in-law on that very first tête-à-tête, as sweat beaded at her brow, and, from the way Nadine was peering at her in naked judgment, most likely on her upper lip, too.

"Ashley is one of my favorite names, actually," she'd said. (This was true, technically. It was indeed a name she'd imagined possibly giving a daughter someday.) "So much more *manly* than Rhett."

And well, there it was. Nadine glared. Margo squirmed, and from that moment forward they tolerated each other under a thin veil of mutual discomfort. Holidays were stilted, gifts were formal, and passive aggression became a new art form. Whenever Margo said or did something that Nadine disapproved of, which was pretty much everything, from the color she painted her kitchen (yellow) to the way she styled her hair (ponytails), Ash would just give his mother an apologetic smile, shrug his shoulders, and say, "She's a Yankee." As if that explained it. And Nadine would pinch her lips as if yes, that did.

Ash. That's what she called him. It was an unsuitable name, really. A little too much in the Rhett territory when it came to the image it conjured up. A little too cool for a man who wore flannel pajamas to bed every night, buttoned up to the neck, because the central air made his skin cold but turning it off gave him heat rash.

Well, now she was being mean. But, really, under the circumstances, who could blame her? For ten years she had tolerated the sleep apnea breathing machine that whirred all through the night. She had always refilled his asthma inhalers. Kept a packet of lactose intolerance meds in the zippered inner compartment of her handbag, even taking the trouble to transfer the pack with each season from black leather handbag to navy linen tote, just in case Ash indulged in ice cream, or pizza, or something else that caused...trouble.

She'd been there when he broke his nose the first (and only) time she'd taken him skiing. She'd held his hand when he hyperventilated into a brown paper bag when they removed the packing. She'd nearly hyperventilated herself from the sight of all that gauze. She loved skiing; but she'd given it up for Ash.

She'd stood by him. Through thick and through thin. Through ups and downs. Through good times and bad...

And where had that gotten her?

Nowhere. All these years later, she was moving backward, not forward. She was moving home.

But only temporarily.

Well now, she was feeling sorry for herself again, and that wasn't good. Twelve hours ago, she'd felt angry. Angry to the bone. But somewhere after the Mason-Dixon, that rage had tempered to sadness and self-pity, and that just wouldn't do. Especially when she'd eaten the last of the chips from the family-sized bag she'd purchased at a truck stop in Maryland.

Margo sighed as she pulled into a gas station off the highway and parked behind a tired-looking tan Jeep with New Hampshire plates. *Almost home*, she thought, feeling suddenly queasy.

There was a chill in the air when she stepped out of the car, despite it only being late September. She rubbed her arms, started the pump, and propped the nozzle in the tank. She'd been driving all night with only a few stops for gas and food; a good cup of hot coffee would settle her stomach, give her the boost she'd inevitably need when she arrived in Oyster Bay. With some explaining to do.

The realization that she was closer to Maine than she was to South Carolina made her frown. She'd actually done it. Packed her bags and left. Left behind her husband, her friends, her career, her house. Her *life*. She'd never again linger at the round, walnut table on Sunday mornings, sipping her coffee and reading the newspaper. She'd never again go to her Tuesday yoga class or her Thursday Pilates class (not that she minded skipping that one, per se—the instructor was far too intense for her liking). She wouldn't eat breakfast at the Peachtree Café or dinner at Froggy's. She'd never again taste that French onion soup that only Chef Pierre could make so right.

Her hair would never again be trimmed by Justine, who knew exactly how Margo liked it (at the shoulder, no layers, no product up-selling on the way out the door), and she'd never again dry her nails under the fan at Belle Femme, the one treat she allowed herself weekly for the sake of professional appearances.

She'd never again take her morning coffee into her studio above the garage, and she would probably never see which fabric Stacy Bittman had chosen for her living room drapes. They'd gone back and forth on this for six months, with Stacy never quite able to decide between the

Jacquard paisley or the damask, and now Margo would never know the outcome. She supposed it was fortuitous that business had been slow lately and that she'd just wrapped up the Morley project: a six-bedroom McMansion and owner with carte blanche. It had been Margo's dream project—she'd selected every object in the home, from the ottomans to the rugs to the cutlery. That project had earned her a name in town. Cindi Morley had hinted more than once that she'd be referring Margo's services to all her friends. So much for that.

Margo pulled open the door and wandered through the cramped aisles to the back of the station's convenience store, trying not to touch anything. No coffee, unless she wanted to ask for a fresh brew and wait. It was just as well. She'd probably spill it on herself. Her hands were shaky from lack of sleep, and every time her phone pinged, she jumped. Instead she walked to the soda machine, plucked the largest paper cup from the stack, questioning only briefly if it would fit in her console's cup holder, added ice, and then pressed it firmly against the lever until the liquid reached the rim. Feeling rebellious, she took a sloppy sip from the edge before topping it off again. She was just pressing the plastic lid on tight with the weight of her palm when the corner of her eye latched onto some generic-brand hand pies stacked neatly above the white sandwich bread and single rolls of toilet paper, and her heart started to flutter in a way she didn't think it could anymore.

In a way it never did for Ash. Not truly. Not the way it had for…well.

It wasn't that Ash wasn't handsome. He was, in that classic, clean-cut, preppy way. Tall and lean, with nut brown hair and glasses, he was the kind of man who wrote three checks a year to charity, who golfed once a month to keep up his game, and who read the morning paper, every morning, in strict silence. It wasn't that she hadn't loved Ash. After all, you didn't live with someone for nearly a third of your life without loving them, did you? It was just that Ash was what some might call a safe bet. Ash was responsible and reliable.

But now Ash was banging a second-year law student named Candace. *His* student. Something she knew only once she'd gotten home yesterday and scoured first the faculty directory and then, with dread, the student registry. Candace wore a string of pearls over a bright pink twinset and had blonde, shoulder-length hair that bounced when she walked. Her teeth were unnaturally white and she had a *dimple,* for God's sake. Margo knew all this because she followed him. That's right. Yesterday afternoon. She had just wrapped up the Morley project and thought she'd stop by to see if he wanted to cut out a little early, maybe even celebrate a little, but he'd been too busy, he said. Papers to grade, he explained, with an apologetic smile and an offer to take her to Froggy's for dinner that weekend instead. She'd left, without a kiss good-bye, not even a peck, and maybe this was the trouble. She'd instead walked to the car, made an appointment for a manicure she never did make it to, and then, right before she backed out of her spot, caught a glimpse of Ash in her rearview mirror, exiting the building. She'd assumed he had changed his mind, so she waited. Waited and then watched as her husband smiled and laughed as he met up with a woman close to ten years her junior, pulled her into his car, and kissed her. Hard. Kissed her in a way he had never kissed Margo. Or at least hadn't kissed her in a very long time.

Margo reached up to touch her lip and then tugged it away. She eyed the snack section again, feeling her stomach rumble. Hell, she deserved it. Some women got flowers and jewelry, and Margo got junk food. She reached for an apple pie and then, because there seemed to be such little point in dieting right now, another. There was a thin layer of dust on the wrappers, but considering how the day was going, she didn't even care.

Margo walked to the cashier, took out her wallet from her bag, and used it as an excuse to check her phone. Nothing. Her heart dropped, even though she knew it shouldn't.

The first apple pie was in her mouth before she even made it back to the car. She finished it entirely and shamelessly licked her fingers clean, only idly considering that she had just handled money, before pulling her phone from her pocket again and doing a few rough calculations.

It was barely nine o'clock. If traffic cooperated, she'd

be in Oyster Bay by ten. Mimi would fix her a plate of pancakes with fresh maple syrup that only seemed to exist in her grandmother's house, brew her some proper coffee that she always served up in her best china, breakfast, lunch, or dinner. They'd sit and chat and Margo would tell her what happened, or maybe she wouldn't. Maybe she'd go to lie down in her old bedroom instead, fall into her soft bed and sleep the day away and pretend that nothing was wrong and everything was all right and that somehow it would all be okay.

The thought was so appealing that she tossed the second apple pie in the trash and set the gas pump back on its hook, smiling for the first time since she'd cackled, rather maniacally, as she'd floored it out of her driveway, a handful of her belongings in the trunk. Ash none the wiser. Yet.

Home in an hour. See, this wasn't so bad, was it?

*

Fifty-nine minutes later, Margo cursed under her breath and eyed the blue and red flashing lights in her rearview mirror. The road into Oyster Bay rarely got busy on weekdays, aside from Friday afternoons, when people came in from Boston or Hartford in droves, eager for a change of scenery and the feeling of sand between their toes. She pushed on the brake pedal, but it was no use. There wasn't another soul on the road. They were coming for her.

Sighing, she pulled to a stop. Felt the prickle of tears at

the back of her eyes, and wondered if now was the time to release them again. She wasn't a fan of using charm or pity to get her way (that was more in her sister Abby's territory), but considering the fact that her husband—her lying, cheating husband—still hadn't called to see where she was or if she was even still alive, she might deserve a little slack.

She cut the engine and reached for the glove box, assuming that all the necessary paperwork would be in there and relieved to see that it was. She felt a little pang, of affection, or fondness, or something else equally inappropriate. She put it firmly in its place. So Ash was good at taking care of these things. Insurance, registration, AAA memberships. He took care of his share, she took care of hers, like making sure he always had his favorite cereal in the pantry, or that the linens were changed every week: things that would never cross Ash's mind. But soon she'd be taking care of both their parts. Things she hadn't even thought about, because she never had to before. Did she even know how to access half of their accounts? Of course not.

She'd taken her life for granted. Gotten comfortable.

Gotten foolish, was more like it.

The cop car was behind her now. Maine plates. Lights still flashing, hell bent on letting anyone who dared to come along know that she was in trouble. Her cheeks flamed with heat. This wasn't like her. She'd been a straight-A student. Gotten a full scholarship to college.

She was a professional.

Margo Harper didn't get pulled over for traffic violations. But then, Margo Harper didn't lick her fingers clean after hanging out in truck stops, either.

She slunk back in her seat and eyed the flashing blue lights through the side mirror, hoping the officer was at least friendly, not a hard ass, considering she had out of town plates. She knew the reputation tourists had around here. They drank too much, lingered a little too long at the tables on Main Street, after the bill had been paid and the wine drunk. They were carefree, happy, maybe even a little irresponsible. And they drove too fast on their way into town. A little slower on their way out.

She frowned. Had she even been speeding? With no other cars to help gauge her pace, she hadn't bothered to check.

Now the cop car door was opening. One foot emerged in the form of a black leather boot. Margo snatched her handbag from the passenger seat. Well, crap. Best to get the humiliation over with.

She rolled down her window, halfway, and slid her South Carolina driver's license through the space, uttering a string of explanations and excuses as she did so. She waited for a response, a reprimand, something. But there was nothing but silence.

Finally, because she had been staring at the steering wheel all this time, barely stopping for a breath, and probably qualifying herself for some kind of test that would require her to touch her nose and stand on one foot, she closed her mouth firmly and turned to look at the officer.

And there it was. The ultimate punishment. No ticket, no matter the fine, could top this moment.

It was Eddie. Eddie Boyd. The same Eddie who had kissed her in the park one crisp fall day and made her believe that anything was possible. The same Eddie who had left town fifteen years ago with a grin on his face and promises he never made good on. She knew his voice. His laugh. The shape of his nose and the curve of his smile. Even with the aviator shades, she'd recognize that face anywhere.

To her disappointment, he didn't look half as surprised as she was to see him.

"Eddie." She licked her lips and ran a palm over her hair only to realize it was pulled into a ponytail, or at least, half of it was. Damn it. No doubt she looked the wreck that she felt. There were probably smudges of mascara under her eyes too from all that crying in the bathroom of that greasy all-night diner she'd stopped at somewhere in Virginia. It would be too strange to pull her sunglasses down now. Too...suspicious.

"Margo Harper." He shook his head, chuckling softly, the sound of it making something in her chest pull a little tighter than it should. "What brings you to town?"

Shouldn't she be saying that? But from the uniform, the answer would be obvious.

Her heart was pounding so loudly she was almost

convinced that he could hear it. Eddie was supposed to be gone. Long gone.

"I didn't realize you'd moved back," she managed. Curse her sisters. Couldn't one of them have mentioned this?

"Only recently," he said. More silence. He'd always been good at that. "You in town for long?"

As if she'd be telling him the details of her arrival. He'd have to arrest her first. Put her under oath. No way would he be finding out that her fairy-tale ending had imploded thanks to a girl named Candy.

"Visiting family," she said, hoping her smile passed for sincere. She didn't want to smile at Eddie. Didn't want to see him or speak to him, for that matter. When she was tucked away in Charleston, she didn't have to worry about unfortunate run-ins with the Boyd family or with reminders of Eddie. But Oyster Bay was small. Too small. So small that she could still see the welcome sign in her rearview mirror. And here he was. Her past. Her everything. Once.

"So." She cleared her throat. "You're a cop now?"

He patted his badge. "Well, it's a little early for Halloween."

She didn't laugh. Her smile had waned. "A cop. How ironic."

His eyes narrowed. "What's that supposed to mean?"

"I seem to recall you getting into your fair bit of trouble once upon a time." A fair bit was putting it mildly.

He gave a lopsided grin. He was so good at those. "We were kids back then. That was half a lifetime ago."

Then why did it feel like yesterday that they'd sat on the sand, holding hands, walking home from school and stopping for a snack that stretched out for hours, not wanting to ever part? Margo frowned, knowing all at once that it had been a mistake to come back to Oyster Bay. Being here, it felt like no time had passed at all. That she hadn't grown up, gotten married, moved a thousand miles away and made a life for herself. Being here, she was still Margo Jane Harper. Middle daughter. Peacekeeper. Daydreamer. Girlfriend of bad boy Eddie Boyd.

The boy who'd left town. And left her.

And here they were. Silence stretched between them, whether for lack of words or nostalgia, Margo couldn't be sure. How many times had she dared to hope, that somehow, someway, they would end up together? That he'd track her down, find her, the way he'd promised her so many times?

Well. It was time to get back on track.

"I didn't realize I had done anything that warranted being pulled over," she said. *Just give me the ticket,* she thought. *Slap my wrist and let me be on my not so merry way.*

"Do you know how fast you were going back there?" he asked, all official and stern.

Please.

She didn't have a clue how fast she had been driving, actually, so she just shrugged.

"Forty." He said it gravely, like it was one hundred forty.

"That doesn't seem very fast to me." Really, who was *he* to talk? Didn't he remember the time he "borrowed" his cousin Nick's Corvette, took her on the back roads, and pushed the speed limit to ninety, until her palms had nail impressions embedded in the skin, despite the way she'd howled in laughter?

"In a thirty-mile zone," he said flatly.

"Thirty!" Margo started to protest and then stopped. She wasn't going to argue with Eddie about the speed limit, or a sign she didn't see, or about the fact that last time she'd been in Oyster Bay, the speed limit had most certainly been forty on this road. There were many things she could argue about with him instead.

"It changed over a mile back. Village-wide policy."

She raised an eyebrow. "New policy?"

He didn't give in. Instead he looked away, giving her a full view of his profile. His straight nose, the slope of his chin. That mouth. God, she'd memorized that face once. Then banished it.

Now it was her turn to look away. She wanted to go, turn the car around and leave. But she couldn't go. Not until he said she could. He was the law now, after all. Or lack of sleep had finally caught up with her and she was officially hallucinating. Really, that seemed like a more realistic scenario.

"I'll let you go with a warning—"

She should be grateful, she knew, but instead she felt

something sputtering to the surface. "A warning." Who did he think he was, her father? This was Eddie. A man who skipped school more days than he went, who never drove within ten miles of the speed limit. A man who had been kicked out of Oyster Bay and sent to juvie to clean up his act.

Well. It looked like he'd kept one promise.

"Thank you." She struggled to form the words. "I should probably let you get back to arresting the real criminals in town."

She went to buckle her seatbelt, but it was already fastened. Awkward.

His mouth quirked. "Eager to get back to town, eh?"

She gave him a long look before sliding her sunglasses down and turning the key in the ignition. "You have no idea."

Chapter Two

Margo gripped the steering wheel a little tighter, barely taking in the sights of Oyster Bay's shops and restaurants as she approached the town center. Eddie Boyd. Her Eddie. Her first dance. First kiss. First heartbreak.

She never thought she'd see him again. With time, she hadn't wanted to see him again. Still didn't. But now she had. And she might again. And then what?

Her mouth felt dry. Nothing good would come from seeing Eddie again. She was a married woman. Well, technically. And he was... She frowned. Was Eddie married? Was that what had brought him back to Oyster Bay? She hadn't checked his hand for a ring. She'd been too shell-shocked to process the fact that she was speaking to him at all, again, after all these years.

She didn't like thinking back on that last summer together, when they spent the afternoons combing the beach, hand in hand, making all sorts of plans that would never happen. She was working as a babysitter that summer, her charges were two little hellions named Oscar and Camille Hodges, towheaded twins that seemed to love nothing more than to fight with each other or get a rise out of her, their mischief ranging from locking each other in various bedrooms and hiding the keys, to once, when Margo dared to turn her back to take a delivery at the door, Oscar cutting off Camille's long golden braid. By the time their mother returned from the job she'd professed to taking "for her sanity," Margo was exhausted, too tired to eat, much less go out with friends. But five minutes with Eddie was all it took to turn her day around. "I hope those two haven't turned you off kids someday," Eddie would joke, and Margo's heart would swell with the possibility that loomed in their future. Endless days together, just the two of them, and then...

And then nothing. They were supposed to graduate high school, maybe go to Boston or New York, somewhere far from Oyster Bay where they could avoid the gossip and the prying eyes and the rumors that seemed to float around about Eddie's past—the life he'd lived before he came to live with his aunt and uncle in this small town. Eddie hated the speculation, the feeling that all eyes were on him, and the wisecracks the kids would make in their quest for information. They'd get an apartment, nothing fancy, and get jobs while Margo went to art school at night. They'd spend weekends walking through their new town, making it their own, dreaming of all that was yet to come.

Instead, after a school yard fight the fall of senior year, Eddie had gone to juvie. And that, as they said, was that.

Only it didn't end there, at least not for her. For six months after he'd left, she wrote letters, checking the box every day for a reply. She tried to call the facility he'd been sent to, only to be told each time that he was unavailable. She applied to colleges at her parents' insistence, and when the full scholarship to Georgetown arrived, she knew she couldn't turn it down. She left for DC a year after Eddie had left, and the first weekend in her new city, she'd borrowed her roommate's car to drive to the detention center in New Jersey, only to be told that Eddie had aged out. Of course. He was eighteen after all. They couldn't provide a new address, and his aunt and uncle back in Oyster Bay knew nothing of his whereabouts. Eddie Boyd was gone.

And now, all these years later, he was back.

She rolled to a stop at the intersection of Gull and Main, watching impassively as people she didn't recognize crossed the street. It was September, and it was Wednesday, meaning these were locals, not tourists. She should know them. At least some of them.

But there was only one person she ever looked for when she came to Oyster Bay—which wasn't often. One face she still scanned for in every crowd; it was habit by now. The need for answers, for understanding. And now she'd seen it. Really, that should be the end of it. Instead, it opened more questions, more confusion. Eddie Boyd. A cop?

She supposed she would have known this if she'd asked one of her sisters. But she'd been a married woman. A happily married woman, or at least happy enough. It would be unseemly to ask outright about an old boyfriend. It was ancient history. They were kids, as Eddie had pointed out. And now Eddie, the Eddie who loved jumping on his motorcycle and speeding through town, no helmet or jacket, laughing until she screamed and hugged his waist a little tighter, was a cop.

And she was a divorcee. Almost.

She didn't know which outcome was more ironic.

A horn behind her honked, and she jumped. Right. Time to focus on the road or risk being pulled over again. By Eddie.

Yeah, no thanks. Unless the next words out of his mouth were a big fat apology, she had nothing more to say to him.

She drove down Main, her eye darting to her speedometer. There was The Lantern, owned by her Uncle Chip, and The Scoop on the corner, where she and her sisters used to ride their bikes to get ice cream on lazy summer afternoons—she and Bridget in the lead, Abby trailing behind.

She pulled onto Shoreline Road, without even having to think about it, knowing every curve and tree as if she'd just seen it yesterday, not coming up on two years this Thanksgiving. She frowned, doing a quick calculation. Make that three years. When she first moved away for college, she'd visited more often, but after Bridget got married and Abby went off to college and then their parents died, well... Sometimes it was easier to focus on the life she had, the home she'd built. With her cheating bastard of a husband.

Mimi's house was just around the corner now, impossible to miss, even if it wasn't her childhood home, and her father's before that. The Harper house was one of the prettiest in all of Oyster Bay, most people in town would quickly agree. It was large enough to comfortably house three children, which is why, perhaps, Mimi felt it was more suitable for her parents' young family than just an aging widow, with white-painted cedar siding and big bay windows and a huge span of cool green grass that led right up to the sandy shore.

Margo eased off the gas, wanting to linger on the sight as the old Victorian came into view. She stopped, stared at it, felt the stress of the drive roll off her shoulders like waves on the sand. She could close her eyes and picture it, room by room, right down to the knickknacks on the bookshelves and the worn floorboards in her bedroom, but today she didn't have to. The old wooden swing that hung from the branches of the big tree on the front lawn swung in the breeze, and if she tried hard enough, she could almost remember the sensation of flying, higher and higher, until she sometimes thought she could let go and drift all the way out to the sea if she really tried hard enough.

She let her gaze linger on the swing, the memory of her father pushing her back, Abby whining that it was her turn soon, and she smiled against the tug in her chest. A seagull swooped past, and she followed it, glancing at the front of the property.

And that was when she saw it. The hard plastic sign blowing in the breeze.

Her childhood home was for sale.

*

The gravel crunched under her feet as she walked up the driveway toward the stone path that led to the house's wraparound porch. Her heart was racing as she reached the steps, frowning when she noticed the chipped paint on the porch railing. Under normal circumstances, she'd offer to touch it up, or make a call to Freddy, the handyman who had worked on the house for as far back as she could remember, doing anything from fixing broken window sashes to installing a new light fixture after Abby had broken the dining room chandelier playing Tarzan when she was five. He whistled while he worked and always charged less than he should, refusing fair pay no matter how much Mimi or Margo's mother insisted. Eventually, they always reached a compromise:

his quoted price plus an invitation to dinner that night. Freddy loved a home-cooked meal, and he wasn't shy with his praise, which pleased Mimi to no end.

It wasn't until Margo was older that she realized Freddy was a bachelor, with no family of his own at all. And that a night sitting at her family's dinner table meant more to him than an extra fifty bucks.

"We're lucky," her mother had said, whenever Freddy left. "Not everyone has what we have."

And now...now what did Margo have?

For all she knew the sale was already pending. A new buyer all lined up. Someone eager to come in and repaint and strip floors and gut the kitchen where her mother used to make cookies, and her father would dance with them, sliding around in socks, letting them stand on his feet as he moved to the box step. All those memories. All they had left. Gone. All under the hand of her own sister.

Margo eyed the FOR SALE sign critically.

Bridget Harper. Well. She'd just have to talk to Mimi about this.

With a heavy heart, Margo rang the bell, wondering now if she should have called before dropping by. When no one answered, she pressed her nose to the glass, relieved to see the furniture still in place. Maybe Mimi was out back having her morning coffee. Of course! It was her favorite spot three seasons of the year; even when the leaves were gone, she'd drape a blanket over her shoulders, saying she never grew tired of the view of the waves crashing against the rocks that lined the shore.

But Mimi wasn't out back, and her favorite rocking chair wasn't either. Margo frowned, and tried the set of French doors that led into the kitchen. Locked. Hurrying, she went back around to the front of the house, but that door had one of those intimidating-looking lock boxes on it, no doubt installed by Bridget in hopes of several showings.

Margo pulled her phone from her back pocket, suddenly realizing that she hadn't checked it since the gas station in New Hampshire. She licked her lips, taking her time in flipping it over and lighting up the screen. Blank. No calls. No texts. Ash would surely have recognized her absence by now. If he was smart, he would have even seen that a few suitcases were missing. Their best suitcases, including the one he preferred to use for his annual conference trips.

Now she wondered what really transpired on those trips. If his indiscretions were limited to one woman, or if this was just his style.

She should have left a note. Crystal clear: *Ash, I'm leaving you.* Really, what else was there to say?

A smile curled her mouth. She could think of several other things to say, but she was a lady.

She supposed Mimi could be in town. She liked to buy fresh flowers, but she usually did that on Sunday, for the start of each week. Margo supposed she could drive around, look for her.

Or she could call her sister. See what the hell was going on.

With that, Margo walked over to the FOR SALE sign and dialed the listed number, bypassing Bridget's cell phone number that was stored in her phone, and going straight to her direct office line.

"Bridget Harper," her sister answered a moment later.

"Bridget." God, it felt good to hear a familiar voice. So good that Margo's throat felt tight. "It's me. Margo."

There was a pause. "Margo! Is everything okay?" A strange reaction, but not completely, considering how much time seemed to lapse between their calls.

For a moment Margo had the urge to tell her sister everything, to let it all come pouring out of her like a flood, but she stopped herself. Now wasn't the time.

"I think I'm the one who should be asking you that," Margo said. "I'm staring at a FOR SALE sign in front of our house."

"You're home? In Oyster Bay?" Another pause, this one shorter. "Why?"

Well, that was a loaded question. "Why is our house for sale?"

"I didn't know you were coming home," Bridget replied, again dodging the topic.

Margo was losing patience. "Well, I am home. I drove all night and I really need a cup of coffee and a hot shower. Mimi isn't home. Can you give me the code to the lock box?"

"I'll be there in ten minutes," Bridget said instead, and hung up without another word.

Margo shoved the phone back into her pocket. The wind was picking up and a chill cut through the thin sleeves of her shirt. She walked back to the car to wait, an unsettling feeling creeping over her as she wiped the chip crumbs from the driver's seat and sat down. Why did she have the distinct impression that there was more to Bridget's sudden urgency than just a concerned sister?

*

Crap. Bridget pushed back her chair and stood. She smoothed her skirt and took one last sip of coffee from her "World's Best Mom" mug. Cold. No time for a refill either. She had more important matters than feeling perky, or at least mildly awake. It was ten thirty and she'd been up for five and a half hours. Some people, like her youngest sister Abby, a lifelong student and professional job hopper, were probably just now pouring their first cup of coffee, not swallowing the dregs of their fourth.

Right. Cold coffee. Then over to the house. Then the big meeting.

She set a hand to her stomach to settle her nerves. Ian Fowler, in search of an oceanfront vacation home, was at this very moment driving up from Manhattan to tour the house. Everything was riding on this meeting going well. And Margo stood to ruin it all.

Well, not on her watch.

Grabbing her handbag, Bridget crammed in her notebook and listing sheets, cell phone, and a few extra business cards, then fished for her keys. They were never where they should be, which was in the interior pocket of her bag. Instead they were in random places like coat pockets, desk drawers, sometimes the pantry, or once, the bathroom medicine cabinet. Her mind was too busy. She had too many thoughts spinning at all times. Too many worries fighting for attention; too many responsibilities to keep track of, like remembering to schedule her fall conference with Emma's teacher. And remembering to inform her ex of the time. Not that he'd show up. No, unlike her, Ryan was too busy for everyday responsibilities like school events or making sure that lunch was packed and homework checked.

Her fingers touched something metal. Good.

"Off to the big meeting?" Her colleague and "work husband" Jeffrey popped his head out of his doorway, tie a bit askew, as she hurried to the door.

"Not yet," she said, slowing her step. She supposed her sister could wait a minute or two. "Margo's in town. She's at the house," she added.

"Oh." Jeffrey was late on the uptake. "Oh," he repeated with more meaning, his eyes widening. He ran a hand over his prematurely balding head and grimaced.

"Exactly," Bridget said, lips thinning. She'd meant to tell her sister about the latest developments, and she would have eventually. But they rarely talked on the phone, and Margo was so removed from family matters and decisions that by luck of birth order had fallen on Bridget's shoulders, that it hadn't been forefront in her mind. She'd been more concerned with handling Mimi, the house, trying to build a career while making sure her daughter had a costume sewn in time for Oyster Bay's summer children's theatre auditions for Peter Pan than keeping Margo in the loop.

Besides, didn't the phone work both ways? If Margo had called between last Christmas and now, Bridget would have gladly filled her in on everything, maybe even gotten a little help out of it, or at least some emotional support.

"Good luck," Jeffrey said, giving her a pat on the arm.

Bridget managed to smile. Whether the luck was for her big meeting or managing her sister, she wasn't sure. Either way, she'd take it.

"And before I forget, Trish wanted me to see if you wanted to come over Saturday night. Nothing fancy. Just us and a few friends."

If by "a few friends" he meant another single father with three rowdy kids in need of a stepmother to handle the laundry and cooking, she'd have to pass. "I'll check my calendar," she said with a smile, then remembered that this Saturday was Ryan's night with Emma, and what else did she have to do with her time?

Well, other than laundry and errands.

Her heart felt heavy as she walked to the car. Life could have been so much easier if she had a Jeffrey to come home to. Jeffrey was the type of father who took his two kids out for ice cream, just because; the type of father who coached Little League and read bedtime stories, with all the voices.

Emma had never known a father like that, and as her mother, Bridget could never forgive herself for this.

She could have picked a guy like Jeffrey McDowell. Heck, she'd gone to school with him. And he had asked her to the spring dance junior year. But no, she had to pick the exciting guy. The slick charmer with the wide grin and twinkling eyes. The guy who liked to have a good time and show her a good time. The guy who didn't want to settle down, not really. The guy who just wanted to do his thing and was still doing it.

She should have followed in her sister's footsteps. Married a guy like Ash.

Just thinking of her sister's reaction made Bridget anxious. Still, once Margo recovered from the shock, she'd understand. Maybe she'd even offer to help a bit. The place needed sprucing up, and God knew that Abby wasn't good for so much as lifting a box.

Bridget drove to the house on autopilot. Down Main, right on Dune, then two miles down Shoreline, Oyster Bay's scenic stretch. This was where the big houses were—the crown jewels in the real estate world. And she had a listing.

Sure, it was her childhood home, but it was a listing all the same. And the sale would certainly be noted, hopefully leading to more prestigious clients down the road. The locals rarely uprooted, but Oyster Bay never tired of those in search of a summer getaway.

Bridget pulled onto the driveway, fighting the wave of nostalgia that still hit her every time she saw the house. A silver SUV was parked at the end; Margo was leaning against the hood. Her dark hair was pulled back in a ponytail and she was wearing a three-quarter sleeved cotton top over her jeans—attire completely inappropriate for Maine this far into September.

"Aren't you cold?" Bridget asked by way of hello, as she climbed out of her own vehicle, her father's ancient Mercedes she'd foolishly hoped would send the right kind of image to potential clients, if it didn't break down while she was driving them around town instead. You know, the one that said, "See? I'm successful, not struggling to pay rent and keep my kid in ballet lessons."

"It beats sitting in the car," Margo said. "I've been driving all night."

Bridget noticed that Margo seemed to be alone. Usually Ash joined her on these rare visits. "Why the last-minute trip?" And why now? Why, why? It had been years since Margo deigned to come back to Maine, and now, right when an offer on the house was nearly within her grasp, Margo was here to mess everything up.

Margo just grinned, but it seemed a little strained. "Don't I at least get a hug?"

Bridget felt her shoulders relax. She really needed to lighten up. This was her sister. Her sister! She was such a wreck over her afternoon meeting that she was jumpy.

She walked over and gave her sister a hug. Tugged her ponytail the way she used to as a kid, only back then it bothered Margo. A lot. "Welcome home."

Margo was frowning when she pulled away. "This isn't the homecoming I was expecting." She tipped her head, locking Bridget's wary gaze. "Mimi's selling the house? But…this is our home."

"We've all flown the nest, Margo." Bridget recited the lines she'd mentally rehearsed on the drive over. "Emma and I are across town. Abby is too. And you have a life somewhere else."

Margo looked resigned. "But where will she go?"

Bridget enjoyed one last moment of silence. Here it came. "Mimi lives in Serenity Hills now."

"Serenity Hills!"

Ah, yes, there it was. The predictable reaction. One she'd deep down been avoiding by not picking up the phone and keeping her sister informed. Bridget stayed firm. "That's right. Serenity Hills. It's the best place for her, really. This house was too big for a woman of her age, with no help."

"We could have hired her some help," Margo scolded.

"We?" Now this was rich. Bridget crossed her arms. "I'm a single mother on a fixed income. Abby can't hold down a job. Chip is Mom's brother, not Dad's, and this isn't his family responsibility. So that would leave you."

Margo crossed her arms. "You should have called me."

"Maybe you should have called Mimi," Bridget shot back, instantly regretting her words. There was truth in them, and she was just defending herself, but the hurt in her sister's eyes made her ashamed. "Look. Serenity Hills is a good place for her."

Margo didn't look convinced. "We used to threaten to dump each other in Serenity Hills someday."

True, very true, but now they were adults. Now they understood the realities of life. At least she did.

Bridget shifted the weight on her feet, feeling uncomfortable. It hadn't been an easy winter for any of them, with Mimi's declining health and the endless worry about something happening to her when she was alone in the big house. Decisions had to be made. Difficult ones. And as usual, she'd been the one to make them. Alone.

Never had she missed her parents more. They'd been gone for eight years, but the pain was always there, lurking just below the surface. At trying times, she felt their loss on a deeper level, imagining how much comfort they could have brought her if they were still here. Sometimes it was just a hug that she needed, or the sound of her father's laughter. Other times, like recently, it was support. Someone to deal with the big problems, someone to ease the burden that came with trying to please everyone and feeling like all you ever did was let them all down instead.

"Serenity Hills is the best place for her," she said more firmly.

"I wish I'd been consulted," Margo said, shaking her head.

"It wouldn't have made a difference. I'm here. I see what's going on."

Margo blinked, then looked away, out to the stretch of lawn that met the sea, and back up to the porch. Bridget wavered, seeing the squint in her eyes that was no doubt fighting off tears, and then straightened up. She couldn't afford to be getting sentimental, now. Not when she was showing this house in less than three hours.

"I take it you were planning on staying here," Bridget said gently. "I'd let you stay with me, but we're pretty cramped, and Ryan got the pull-out couch in the divorce."

Margo kicked at the gravel with her shoe. "I understand. I'll go to a hotel."

A hotel. Is that what it was coming to? No more gatherings around the big kitchen table or Christmas carols in the parlor. From now on, when Margo came to visit for holidays, she'd be staying at the stuffy Oyster Bay Hotel.

Bridget couldn't bear it. "How long are you in town for?"

Margo shrugged. "A week. Maybe more." She looked back down at her feet, and Bridget narrowed her gaze. That was an odd response, and it wasn't like Margo to be so free with her time. She swept around, just in case she'd missed Ash somewhere. But no, it was clear that her sister was alone. And in Oyster Bay for an undetermined amount of time. Interesting.

"Well, I know of a weekly rental that's available." It was Jeffrey's listing, and he was having a hell of a time filling it after Labor Day. "It's tastefully furnished, waterfront. Since it's off season the rent is lower. Probably less expensive than the hotel, and you'd have your own kitchen."

Margo's eyes sparked for the first time since Bridget had stepped out of her car. "I'll take it."

Bridget smiled. "Should I put you down for a week?"

Margo's eyes drifted. "Oh. Maybe two?"

Bridget studied her sister, but decided against saying anything. She was probably reading into things, and besides, she had a meeting to prepare for. "Well," Bridget said, as she pulled out her phone. "I doubt there's any other interest. Let's start with one week and take it from there."

A message popped up on her screen. The showing was postponed until Friday. Too much traffic out of Manhattan to get here today, Ian reported.

Bridget felt her heart sink, but only for a moment. This gave her one more day to prepare. And it gave her time this afternoon to settle Margo into the cottage. And maybe figure out what the heck was going on in her sister's life…and why she had returned to Oyster Bay.

Chapter Three

The gulls were calling the next morning when Margo woke up, fully clothed, on top of the white duvet, the novel she'd been reading the night before abandoned next to her. Sunlight poured in through the linen curtains that draped across the tall windows, and she didn't need a watch to know she'd slept way past her usual six o'clock wake up time.

She fumbled her hand along the nightstand in search of her phone, which she'd silenced the evening before, so she didn't have to continue to sit and wait for it to make some sound that would tell her that Ash was looking for her. That Ash cared. Now the top corner of the device was flashing a blue light, and her heart sped up when she saw that she had three new messages.

So maybe he did care. Maybe ten years of her life were

not a complete waste.

Or maybe they were. After all, the man was cheating on her. Who could be sure it was even the first time? She set the phone back down, closing her eyes when she thought of the way he'd kissed that girl. She'd sat in her car, at a safe enough distance, and stared as if it weren't her husband she was watching, but some addictive, trashy television show that she couldn't look away from, even though she knew she should. She sat there, jaw slack, and watched. Didn't get out of her car, march over and pound on the window. Nope. She just sat there and did nothing, until Ash's car moved, and then, well, what choice did she have? She'd followed him. Followed him all the way to the friggin' Holiday Inn Express. And then, because there was nothing more to see, and nothing else to do, she'd gone home and packed.

Well, after she'd taken their wedding photo, ripped it to shreds, and then set the empty sterling silver frame back on the mantle.

What did the messages say? And how would she even reply? Should she even reply at all, or make him sweat a bit?

But then, what if he filed a missing person's report? Got the police involved? That wouldn't be good.

No. It was time to confront him. To tell him what she saw. What she knew. To face the harsh, ugly truth. She squeezed her eyes shut, willing herself not to cry. The heaviness in her chest came from a place she couldn't quite recognize, a strange mixture of sadness and fear, of humiliation and rejection and betrayal.

Would he deny it, spin some story? The man was an obvious liar.

Or maybe...maybe there was a reasonable explanation. She snorted.

Margo sat up, grabbed the phone, and scolded herself. She'd been back in Oyster Bay for less than twenty-four hours and she was right back to how she'd been when she first left it. She was acting like a child. This was a man she had shared a home, a bed, every single dinner with, for ten years. She shouldn't be calculating her responses at this point. This was her husband. In the legal sense.

She tapped on the messages, not even realizing she'd been holding her breath until it escaped from her, in one, pathetic puff. The messages were from Bridget.

Of course.

She took a moment to push Ash away, and set aside the ache in her chest that seemed determined to settle there, the weight of it a constant reminder of her circumstances, and scanned the messages: Bridget wanting to know how the cottage was working out for her; Bridget wondering if she was free to come over for dinner tonight, Abby would be joining; Bridget giving her the visiting hours for Serenity Hills.

Where the spirit goes to die.

Margo flopped back on the bed, half of her wanting to pull the blanket up and stay under it for the rest of the day. But that would be giving in. And she wasn't a napper; couldn't sleep during the day if she tried. She'd visit Mimi. Stay busy. Ash would call. Eventually he'd have to, even if it was to figure out something dumb like how to work the washing machine. Margo cursed good old Nadine for her son's domestic shortcomings and then realized a perk of divorce was never having to see Nadine again.

Yes, eventually he would call. And then, well then she'd what? Tell him it was over? That she wanted a divorce?

Divorce meant more than no longer being with Ash. It meant giving up her life with him. Her career, her home, her Saturday morning trips to the farmers market and her monthly book club meetings where literature was rarely on topic…There would be no more quick errands to the organic grocery store. She'd never again have the luxury of asking Mr. Herring at the dry cleaners on Eighth Street if he could fix the button on one of her shirts, knowing that in the top drawer of his desk he had an entire selection of buttons in every shape and size and that she could rest assured he'd always have a match. No more dinners at Froggy's. No more evenings sitting on her back patio, sipping wine while Ash grilled steaks. That was the part that didn't seem possible.

She sat up and read the messages again. Her fingers hovered over the screen, but she didn't reply. Her sister was trying to make amends, but it hardly made up for not telling her about Mimi or the house. But then, Abby hadn't bothered to tell her either.

She fired off a quick note, thanking Bridget for the cottage and agreeing to dinner, and then went in search of coffee.

The cottage was small, with two bedrooms and a bathroom upstairs, and a bright, open concept living space below that extended onto a white-washed deck that led right onto the sand. She'd picked up some supplies at the grocery store yesterday afternoon, but she'd been too worn out to eat dinner, and now her stomach rumbled. She opened the fridge and surveyed her options; her current mindset in full display in the form of chocolate cake, a few bottles of wine, three tubs of ice cream, and enough chips to feed a frat party.

But she knew what she really wanted to eat; something that could only be found in Oyster Bay. Something worth showering for, worth the willpower it took not to grab the bottle of Sauvignon Blanc by the neck and settle onto the couch for the day.

Thirty minutes later, she was pulling up to Angie's Café, all worries neatly stashed away as she anticipated the taste of her favorite blueberry scone, always made with blueberries straight from Hollow Tree Farm.

"Margo Jane Harper!"

Margo froze in the doorway. Only one person called her by her first and middle name, and that was her former piano teacher, Mrs. Boyd, also known as Eddie's aunt.

Friggin' fabulous.

Margo plastered on her best smile and turned to greet

Lori, always a kind, gentle-natured woman, who led the church choir and taught music at the elementary school one day a week. "Mrs. Boyd! It's so good to see you!" It wasn't entirely untrue. Margo had fond memories of sitting at Mimi's big piano in the bay window, sharing a bench with Mrs. Boyd, who always reached into her pocket and pulled out a wrapped chocolate at the end of each lesson, two if Margo hit all the right notes.

Now Margo hesitated, wondering if she should mention her run-in with Eddie and decided against it. The circumstances didn't exactly shed her in the best light, and besides, she shouldn't be thinking of Eddie at all right now. She should be thinking of Ash. And why he still hadn't called.

And why he was cheating on her. And when he'd stopped loving her.

"Margo!" Lori seemed to reach for a hug but then thought better of it. Things were strained, still, after all these years. "In town for long?"

And there was the loaded question. It wasn't going away, and Margo needed to think of a good response so she wouldn't feel so rattled every time someone asked her this. "I'm between projects with work, so I thought I'd use the time to visit my family."

Fair enough. It had been three years, after all.

"And how is business?"

"Good," Margo replied, but the heaviness in her heart said otherwise. Business had been good. Very good. And it still could be. But that would require going back to Charleston, confronting Ash, or maybe just looking past his indiscretions, hoping they would go away. She frowned. Like that was realistic. Or in her nature.

Instead she was technically unemployed, living in a rental, not even her family home. She couldn't sustain this for long. She'd have to make a decision. And soon.

She sighed. But not today.

"How's Nick?" she asked, and sure enough, Lori beamed.

"He's living in Portland now. He just got a promotion at the bank."

"Nice!" Margo had fond memories of Lori's only child, who was Bridget's age, but never her type. She only had eyes for Ryan back then—who was full of charm and funny stories, and who used to write her songs on his guitar.

"It's still strange to think that you've all grown up." Lori hesitated. "You know, I probably shouldn't be saying this…"

Margo sensed a "but" coming on.

Lori gave an embarrassed smile. "It's silly, but I always thought you and Eddie were going to end up together."

Well, that made two of them. Not that Margo would be admitting as much.

Lori's eyes skirted over the display case. "I'd always hoped things would turn around. Then I worried we'd made the wrong decision in sending him away. But then you went to college and got married, so…I guess everyone moved on." She trailed off, a wan smile on her face.

That wasn't exactly how it had gone, but now wasn't the time to bother with correcting Eddie's aunt. It wouldn't help anyone to point out that it was Eddie who had disappeared, left dozens of letters unanswered, broken Margo's heart, moved on without her and given her no choice but to do the same. And it wouldn't change a damn thing.

"We drifted apart," was all she said. "I've always felt sad about that." That was putting it mildly.

"Well." Lori gave an embarrassed grin. "It's ancient history. I wouldn't even bring it up, except...Well, Eddie's moved back to town. I'm sure he'd love to see you while you're here."

Margo lifted an eyebrow, hating herself for the quickening of her pulse at the thought that she still mattered to Eddie to at all. "I bumped into him, actually, on my way into town." She struggled to find something diplomatic to say. "It certainly brought back a lot of memories."

"I'm sure it did," Lori said, picking up her white bakery box when her name was called. "Well, hopefully you won't be a stranger on your visit. Is your husband with you, too?"

Margo felt her already strained smile pull a little tighter. "No, it's a busy time of year for him. He's a professor and school just went back into session, so it's...just me."

Just me. Is this how it would be from now on? Just her, back where she'd started, still being reminded of the seventeen-year-old girl who'd loved Eddie Boyd and believed in him almost as much as she believed in happy endings? Just her, floating through town, dodging prying questions from the neighbors who had known her since birth, witnessed every school event and transformation, from her first bike ride to her first training bra to her first heartbreak.

There were no secrets in this town. No privacy, no place to hide. It had been Eddie's downfall. Hers too, really.

And this, she thought, as she gathered up her paper bag and coffee cup, was why she'd left Oyster Bay in the first place.

*

Margo had one true memory of Serenity Hills—a shining moment, some might say. Miss Berriman's Dance Studio made an annual appearance at the center, in what Margo now saw clearly as an effort to cheer up the residents, but which she saw at the time as an opportunity to show off her moves and wear a little lipstick.

Margo was about fourteen at the time, dressed in teal blue sequins with matching eye shadow she'd borrowed from her mother's makeup bag. Her cheeks were pink, her lips were red, and her hair was crimped. She was ready.

The performance took place in the Serenity Hills

cafeteria; tables had been cleared and the girls had been reassured the linoleum was no different from the dance studio floor.

"Smile!" Miss Berriman had cried out from her post near the industrial-sized freezer, as she shooed the line out the kitchen door.

Margo had smiled against her nerves, but when she saw the white-haired men in the front row smiling back, it made things a little easier. They clapped to the music. A few even winked. Her confidence was so high by the end of the night that she signed herself up for the high school talent show the very next day, and a week later shimmied on stage to perform her group tap routine solo in front of the entire freshman class. She'd grinned cheekily at the boys in the front row, but instead of indulging her the way the men at the old folks home had, they'd just giggled and jabbed each other in the ribs, a few even pointed.

Margo looked down at her leotard and bare legs and felt a cold wash of fear come over her. She finished the routine and ran off the stage, barely holding back her tears.

She'd never performed again. But she'd never forgotten the reception she had at Serenity Hills either. Or the fact that the very next morning after the talent show, the new boy in town, Eddie Boyd, had come up to her, told her he liked her performance, and grinned like he meant it.

Now Margo walked by this cafeteria, which, judging

from the Berber carpet, must have undergone a renovation since that blissful night, and stopped at the front desk.

"I'm here to see Margaret Harper," she said.

The woman behind the desk tapped a manicured finger on an open binder next to a vase of what were probably meant to be cheerful looking flowers but instead had the eerie vibe of a funeral arrangement. "All visitors need to sign the log. Mrs. Harper is in room 132. To the left, follow the signs." She went back to reading her magazine, a cheesy tabloid, without another glance in Margo's direction.

Margo fought to control her temper. Was this an example of all the staff, or just one employee? The only thing worse than the thought of her grandmother living here rather than in her beautiful family home was the thought of her not being treated well. Images of late night commercials flooded to the surface. Stories of abuse and neglect and…She blinked back tears that prickled the back of her eyes. She'd jot down the names of some of those attorneys, next time she saw a television ad. Just in case.

"If she's not in her room, just wait for her. Thursdays she goes to the salon," the woman added, before flicking the page.

Margo set the pen on the binder. Salon? Well. Maybe this place wasn't so bad then.

She shifted her handbag straps on her shoulder as she walked toward the hall. Her heart was racing and her stomach was hurting. She tried not to glance into the open doors that lined either side of the passageway. Eyes forward. Find room 132. Talk to Mimi before it's too late. Simple enough. The house hadn't sold—yet. But Margo wasn't taken any chances. She'd have to act quick. With any luck, she'd be loading Mimi into the car in less than an hour.

Room 132 was at the end of the building, a fair distance from the lobby. Margo took this as an immediately good sign that her grandmother was much less dependent than those whose rooms were within shouting distance of the front desk.

Mimi was sitting in her rocking chair—the weather-worn one that used to reside on the back of the wraparound porch. A quilt was around her shoulders and she was stroking what appeared to be a grey stuffed animal.

This wasn't good.

"Mimi?" Suddenly the animal moved. "Jesus!" Margo jumped. "What the hell is that?"

Mimi gave her a reproachful look. "Watch your language, young lady." Then, looking down to stroke the cat fondly, she said, "This is Pudgie."

Pudgie? Margo decided to pick her battles.

"Mimi, are you allowed to have that thing in here?"

Mimi looked at her quizzically. "Of course I'm allowed, Abby. You gave him to me, after all."

Margo felt her heart sink. Of the three Harper girls,

Margo and Abby took after their father, with dark brown hair, green eyes, and a dusting of freckles. But Abby was four years younger and two inches shorter, and coloring aside, they were far from twins.

"I'm Margo," she said gently. She walked forward, tried to reach out for Mimi's hand, but Pudgie gave a hiss of warning, forcing her to snatch it back.

"Margo?" Mimi stared at her until, to Margo's relief, her eyes filled with recognition. "Of course! Margo! Come here and give me a hug, girl." Sensing Margo's hesitation, she gave Pudgie a pat. "Don't worry. He doesn't bite. At least, not too hard."

Crisis averted. It was a simple mistake. Dark hair, green eyes, and it had been nearly three years since her last visit. Mimi had just been surprised to see her. Surely that was all it was.

Careful not to upset Pudgie, she leaned down to give her grandmother a hug, breathing in the smell of peppermint and perfume that brought back a hundred wonderful memories all at once.

"Margo, Margo." Her grandmother shook her head as Margo pulled away. "That's right. You moved down south. Got married to that woman. Ashley."

Margo blinked. "Ash," she said evenly, "is a man."

Mimi didn't look convinced. "No need to protect me," she said with a wink. "I'm not living in the stone age."

"No, really, Mimi. Ashley—Ash—is a man. He's a law professor. Remember our wedding?"

Who could forget it, after all? The church was

enormous, more like a cathedral, and each pew had been anchored by a huge bouquet of roses. The aisle had been lined with a white carpet, and a string quartet had played all of Nadine's favorite songs for the procession...

Mimi squinted for what felt like an unnatural amount of time. "You wore my pearls."

"Yes," Margo exhaled in relief.

Mimi patted the empty visitor chair next to the television. Dutifully, Margo sat down.

"Tell me, how old are you now?"

"I'm thirty-two," Margo said. *And my husband has already left me for a younger woman.*

"Thirty-two! When did that happen?"

Margo hissed out a nervous laugh, hoping against her better judgment that Mimi was making some sort of joke. The last time she'd been in Oyster Bay, Mimi had been full of life, pushing everyone out of the kitchen so she could prepare dinner without being disturbed. Over her famous apple pie, she'd told them stories of the time her son, their father, then just a boy, had brought home a baby snapping turtle and kept it in his room for two months without anyone being aware, until one day Mimi went into his closet and had the surprise of her life.

There was no confusion. Her memories had been as sharp as her mind.

Margo fought back tears. She wanted to cling to her grandmother, ask her to explain. What had happened? How was she to know that last visit would be the last time she'd truly speak to her grandmother at all?

Mimi looked at her sharply. "You old enough to drive?"

Margo didn't like where this was going. "Well, yes."

Mimi slanted her eyes at the door. "Think you could bust me out of here?"

It was what she had come to do, but now Margo didn't know whether to laugh at the irony or cry at the circumstances. "I don't think Bridget would approve."

Mimi waved a hand through the air. "Oh, Bridget never was any fun. You, Abby, you were always fun."

Mimi was right about one thing: Abby was fun. It was Abby who broke into song for every car ride, not caring who was watching, and Abby who danced the night away at every wedding, even if her moves didn't exactly match the music.

But Mimi was very wrong about something else.

"I'm Margo," she said with a smile, but she wasn't sure she could hold the tears back much longer.

Mimi went back to petting Pudgie, and Margo looked around the room for distraction, desperate not to let her grandmother see her cry. There was a single bed that faced the chair on which she sat, and a bedside table that held nothing more than a lamp and two framed photos: one of Mimi on her wedding day, and the other of Margo's parents.

Margo stood and crossed the room to pick up the photo of her parents, taken at the beach, when they couldn't have been much older than Margo was now.

Once there had been a time when she looked at their photo daily, needing to keep them with her, keep their image fresh. Now, she realized with shame that somewhere in the past eight years she'd grown accustomed to life without them, even went for days without thinking of them at all.

It was easier in Charleston, of course. But here in Oyster Bay, there was no avoiding it. Her parents were gone. They'd died in a car accident on a winding road in bad weather. Abby, being the youngest, had taken it the worst. Bridget had taken it in stoic stride—having a newborn baby to focus on had helped. But Margo, well, she was the only one who could escape from it, for a little while at least.

Margo quietly set the frame back on the table and looked over at Mimi, wondering if she remembered the accident, that she'd lost her only son, and hoping, strangely, that Mimi didn't remember it any more than she could remember Margo's name.

"Let's take a walk," Margo said abruptly. The suggestion was made with more enthusiasm than she felt, but she couldn't sit in this room any longer. The memories were weighing down on her, and that cat—she glanced at it, and if she didn't know better, she'd swear it had just narrowed its eyes—that cat was creeping her out. "You can give me a tour."

Mimi sighed. "Not much to show, but fine." She perked up for a moment. "Pudgie likes to be shown off.

He's quite the ladies' man, you know."

The cat seemed to glare at Margo as she helped Mimi into a wheelchair, her chest aching that this is what Mimi's life had come to, and pushed her out the door. So this is what she had to get used to. Mimi wasn't just living in a home. She was also a package deal with a grouchy feline with a silly name.

"Oh, that's a pretty wreath on that door," Margo said, determined to stay cheerful as they moved toward the lobby. "Maybe I should get you one for your door."

Mimi craned her neck to look up at her. "So you're not busting me out? Then where are we going?"

Margo's eyes burned. Mimi was funny and strong and wise. She danced and sang and she belonged to a quilting club. And the woman staring back at her wasn't Mimi. She just looked like Mimi. An old woman with thinning hair and trembling hands and watery eyes.

And somehow, Margo had missed this transition. Somehow, while she was in South Carolina, content in her suburban married life, picking out ottomans and drapes and recommending various drawer pulls for a custom kitchen renovation, Mimi had gotten old. And disappeared.

She cleared her throat, but the lump was still there. "What time is lunch?"

"Why? You planning on staying?" Mimi curled her lip. "Take me to the cafeteria. We'll see what's on the menu."

Margo did as she was told, guiding the wheelchair down the hall. "Pretty flowers," she commented, gesturing to the bouquet on the visitor's desk.

"Those were from Betty LaMore's funeral last Saturday," Mimi said, pinching her lips.

As suspected, Margo thought grimly.

"That hussy Esther Preston is already making a move on Mitch LaMore," Mimi continued. "He's ninety-four and has no one to leave his fortune to now that poor Betty's gone to meet her maker."

"Mimi!" But Margo was laughing as she pushed the wheelchair into the cafeteria, which, from the various posters on the wall, seemed to function as a multi-purpose room. Bingo, arts and crafts, game night, and a special whiteboard with names scribbled all over it. Margo paused for a better look. "The *ultra* conservatives club," she read aloud, and then, with a tut, noticed Mimi's name scrawled at the bottom.

Oh, Mimi. She shook her head and moved them to the back of the room, where a menu was set up on an easel.

"Just what I thought," Mimi said, leaning forward to squint at the large print. "Slop, slop, and more slop."

"Oh, now, it doesn't look so bad!" Margo scanned the items. "I can't remember the last time I had a four-course meal."

"Well, it's hardly the Ritz," Mimi sniffed.

Margo had an idea. "What if I take you to The Lantern one night for dinner? Would you like that?" Even though it was owned by Margo's mother's brother, Mimi had adopted the place as her own.

Mimi looked uncertain. "You'll have to check with the warden, but yes, I would, Abby!"

That settled it then. Abby, or Margo, or whoever it was that Mimi needed her to be would take her to dinner at The Lantern. Uncle Chip would give them the family table and add extra whipped cream to their desserts and keep them distracted with funny stories and a friendly grin. Margo felt better just thinking about it.

She pushed the wheelchair out of the room and down a few more halls. In fairness, it did seem like a nice place. Not the Ritz but…nice.

"I think Pudgie needs a nap before lunch," Mimi said, stifling a yawn.

Margo gave a sad smile. "I'll bring you back to your room, then." Defeat settled over her. Everything was slipping away. Everything had changed.

And shame on her for ever getting comfortable in the first place.

With a heavy heart, she pushed the wheelchair back toward room 132, this time walking more slowly, and daring to look around, to face her new reality. Most of the doors were open, televisions were on, some other residents had guests. In the distance she even heard the sound of a child laughing. She smiled at that, but it slipped from her face when she rounded the bend and saw a man standing in the doorway of another room. Tall and broad shouldered, with nut brown hair that curled ever so slowly at the neck.

She'd know that hairline anywhere. She'd memorized it

freshman year, sitting behind him in algebra, on the days he bothered to show up to class.

Eddie.

What the hell was he doing here? And really, what was he doing back in Oyster Bay at all?

Now wasn't the time to find out.

Heart racing, she swiveled the wheelchair and then realized that there was nowhere else to go, unless she wanted to push Mimi into a janitor's closet. It was tempting.

"What are you doing, girl? Abby! Abby!"

Margo closed her eyes, feeling her face heat, and then glared at the wall, knowing with a sinking feeling that Eddie was probably staring at her backside. Her thirty-two-year-old backside. A far cry from the seventeen-year-old figure she'd once possessed, despite her twice a week Pilates classes and three days of cardio on the stationary bike.

She turned. Eddie's mouth quirked into a grin. But not just any grin. It was that slow, lopsided, mischievous grin that got her into trouble, every time. The kind that didn't need a verbal invitation. That kind of smile that just said…everything.

Margo didn't grin. She didn't smile. She gave a tight nod, gripped the handles of the wheelchair a little tighter, and pushed Mimi and Pudgie back into their room at the end of the hall, where she hid for the next hour, before doing what she did best these days. She fled.

*

There was a box of donuts from Angie's next to the coffeepot when Eddie walked into the station. Normally he tried to avoid sugar as much as he avoided alcohol, but this morning, his self-control was plummeting.

He grabbed a mug and filled it, then stared at his options.

To hell with it. If he was going to eat a donut, it was going to be a good one. And Angie made the best donuts in town.

"Someone's birthday?" he asked Sylvia as he walked to his desk. From the numerous reminders she'd dropped in the past few weeks, he knew for a fact that her birthday wasn't until Saturday.

His partner eyed him with suspicion. "Since when do you eat sweets?"

"Since I came from visiting Ray," he replied evenly.

A look of recognition crossed her face. "Well, don't go reaching for another one. Wouldn't want to mess up your boyish figure."

He laughed, appreciating the way she lightened the otherwise sensitive topic. "Anything come in this morning?"

"It's ten thirty. And this is Oyster Bay, not Philly," she reminded him, as she liked to do whenever he complained about the lack of action. "But I'll tell you what. Next time Damon Padilla calls complaining that his cat climbed up his tree again, I'll let you handle it."

"Wow, thanks," Eddie said, but he was grinning.

"Now, if you'll excuse me, I have a donut to fetch." She pushed herself out of her chair and then sat back down again. "No, I do not have a donut to fetch. I ran on that treadmill for forty-five minutes this morning and I am not going to undo all that hard work with a donut."

"There you go," he said, taking another bite from his own. He powered up his computer and tapped in his password.

Sylvia was watching him, a look of longing taking over her big blue eyes. She pushed a strand of graying hair behind her ear, then licked her bottom lip.

"One donut won't kill you, you know."

"No, but one donut will set me back an entire day," she replied, turning back to her paperwork. She looked up again. "Fifteen pounds per kid. You know what that adds up to?"

Eddie quickly did the math and refrained from comment.

"Got to get my figure back in shape before I'm forty if I'm ever going to be asked out on a date again."

"But you're turning forty this Saturday," Eddie pointed out.

"Exactly," Sylvia said.

He opened his mouth to give her some words of advice, something he'd learned in his several hundred AA meetings, but stopped himself just in time. Sylvia didn't know he was in recovery. All she knew was that he left the force in Philadelphia for a simpler life in Oyster Bay, where he'd spent three and a half years with his aunt and uncle, back when he was just a kid.

That was all she needed to know. That was all anyone needed to know.

"You have big plans for the big day?"

Sylvia looked at him like he was half-crazy. "Other than cooking for my three ingrates?"

He knew she didn't mean it. Those kids were her life. But there was still a hint of something sad in her voice that didn't sit right with him.

"Bobby is old enough to look after the younger two for a few hours, isn't he?"

Sylvia cocked an eyebrow. "Bobby is fifteen. Do you remember what you were like when you were fifteen?"

He did, not that he'd be sharing. When he was fifteen he was awkward and shy and scared and didn't know how to handle any of that. He was the new kid in town, the outsider, and his mysterious background didn't help matters. The only person other than his aunt, uncle, and cousin Nick to go out of their way to make him feel welcome was Margo, and all because he'd sensed she felt the same way, after she'd humiliated herself at the school talent show. He'd shown her a little kindness, and in return…she'd shown him everything. How to trust, open up, how to believe that life could be so much more than the trailer park he'd come from, with his drunk dad and his gambling debts and his temper.

"You think a fifteen-year-old boy is responsible enough to take care of his brothers?" Sylvia was still saying.

Not if Bobby was anything like the boys Eddie had known. Those boys were mean, immature, and determined to get to the dark dirty truth of his past, no matter what it took. He was taunted for being new. Teased for being different. And when things got too bad, instead of walking away, Eddie took the bait. Every time. Because he was fifteen years old, and he didn't know what else to do.

"What about a sitter?"

"I suppose their father could take them for the night. Why?" Now Sylvia looked pleased.

"Dinner's on me this Saturday. You deserve a night out. And you never know, you might end up meeting someone."

"I won't hold my breath," Sylvia said, but she was smiling when she said, "Thank you. And with that, I will cut out all sugar until Saturday. Chip Donovan makes a mean skillet cookie."

Eddie grinned. "I applaud your self-control. And just to make it easier for you, I will not eat this donut in front of you."

"Thank you," she said primly.

He stood, headed toward the conference room, taking his coffee with him, and stood near the window, looking out over the town center as he polished off what was left of his breakfast. He'd been back in Oyster Bay for months, and in all that time, he'd managed to control himself. His emotions, his urges, everything squared up, in place.

And then Margo Harper had to come back.

Chapter Four

In exchange for finding a renter for the cottage, Jeffrey had thrown Bridget a bone: first-time buyers in the market for a starter home.

The only thing better was if he'd tossed her a potential buyer for Mimi's house, but of course those kinds of people were few and far between, and she'd had little interest since she'd listed it last month. Still, it only took one person, and in twenty-four hours Bridget would know if she had a bite. If this lead didn't pan out, the house would likely sit on the market all winter; she'd have to relist it in the spring. It wouldn't be such a problem if the cost of upkeep didn't directly clash with the cost of the retirement home.

Still, deep down she clung to the dream of holding onto her childhood home a little longer. Having one last

Christmas in the front living room. The fire crackling while everyone took turns playing carols on the piano, Emma helping Mimi bake cookies for Santa in the big, white kitchen.

Not an option, she reminded herself firmly, as she pulled off Gull Lane and onto a gravel road that bordered the north side of town. The couple was meeting her at a cozy, three-bedroom Cape that had just come on the market last week, its former owners headed for the eternal sunshine of Florida. When it first popped up on the MLS, Bridget had pored over the photos, imagining herself living in it, knowing it was a big step up from her current situation but still just slightly out of reach. The kitchen was small, but renovated, with a cute little eating nook nestled beside a bay window. She could almost picture Emma doing her homework there while Bridget made dinner, or setting up a swing set in the tree-filled backyard, before Emma grew too old for that sort of play.

Of course, like so many of the homes she had toured for professional reasons, living in one was a long shot for a divorced, single mom. And it had been a long shot back when she was married, too. Sure, they'd been comfortable, living in a rental home that she'd tried to make her own. It was more spacious than her current apartment, and more expensive too, but it still wasn't her own, and Ryan didn't understand that need. The money she'd saved from her part-time college job had gone toward Ryan's restaurant, as had all her earnings at the hotel in town, where she'd worked as an assistant manager for a few years. It was an "investment," he claimed, in "their" future. But Bridget had her doubts. And as much as she had hoped to be proven wrong, she never was. Any profit the restaurant turned went back into the business, and all of Bridget's hopes and dreams got put on the back burner.

Well, no more. She was working hard, building back her savings, even if two steps forward always felt like three steps back lately.

The listing was at the end of the road, tucked neatly between two maple trees whose leaves were just started to turn orange. A young couple (well, everyone felt young compared to her lately) was standing on the front step. Holding hands, God help her.

Bridget eyed her naked ring finger, a habit she couldn't kick even after nearly eight years, and gave herself a quick pep talk, which rarely worked, but it was better than nothing.

It is better to be alone and broke than miserable and comfortable.

Sometimes, like when she saw just how sweet this house was, she questioned that philosophy. After all, Ryan hadn't been that bad, had he?

Strike that. Yes, he had been that bad. And worse.

With a brighter smile than she felt, she climbed out of her car and crossed the brick-paved path to greet her new clients. They parted hands long enough to shake hers.

"New to Oyster Bay?" She'd lived in this town all her

life and thought she knew everyone by now.

"We wanted a fresh start," the wife explained.

Didn't everyone? Problem was, it wasn't as easy as it seemed. When she and Ryan had split up, she told herself it was for the best. That she'd be better off on her own. She imagined a sweet, simple house for her and Emma. Chatty meals at the dinner table. Carefree weekends without all the fighting and arguing that her married life had given her.

So much for that. She worked every weekend she could; if a client wanted to see a house, she had to be available. And as for dinners, by the time she walked in her front door it was all she could do to heat up something from the frozen section so she'd still have time to look over Emma's homework and get her ready for the next school day.

"We're both from small towns, and we like small towns, but…"

Bridget nodded. "I understand. A new place for a new phase." She would have liked that herself. Instead she had the joy of sharing Oyster Bay with her ex. "Oyster Bay is a wonderful community," she said as she punched the code into the lock box on the front door. "The beaches are some of the best in the state, and the town center is very vibrant. I'm happy to recommend some good restaurants, if you'd like."

"We had lunch at Dunley's," the husband said.

At the mention of Ryan's establishment, Bridget could only hope her expression remained neutral. "Well," she managed, pushing open the door. "Let's have a look."

She stood in the front entranceway, imagining what it would be like to kick off her shoes, hang her bag on the hook, and go into the kitchen for a cup of tea. In the eight years since she'd joined Bayside Realty, first in the front office and later, when Emma was school-age, as a real estate agent, she'd walked through dozens of homes, from budget-friendly seasonal rentals in need of a complete rehab to beachfront estates, but this was the first time she'd experienced a feeling of...longing. She'd saved up a lot over the years, pinching and scrimping, and if she had one more year, or one big sale, something like this could maybe be hers. Maybe.

She cleared the thought, forced her eyes away from the arched doorway that led into the living room, and to the listing sheet she held in her hand. "This is a three bedroom, two bath."

"Is the basement finished?" the wife cut in. She pursed her lips as she looked at the adjoining dining room from the hallway where they stood.

"No," Bridget said, sensing the couple's disappointment. "But we can check the ceiling clearance. Older homes like this were built differently than newer construction."

She led them through the living room, gazing wistfully at the brick-framed fireplace with the wide mantle, and back through the hall to the kitchen, which was at least double the size of her apartment's offering, and certainly filled with more charm.

Judging from their silence, the couple didn't seem nearly as impressed as she was.

"Should we go upstairs?" she asked, leading them back into the hallway.

"Actually, I think we've seen enough," said the husband. "We're looking for something more modern."

The wife nodded. "Clean lines."

From her experience, clean lines was code for boring and sterile. Everything a home shouldn't be.

"Okay," she said, trying not to show her disapproval. Every sale counted, and this one could go toward that summer camp Emma was already hoping to attend next year. "I'll go back to the office and see what I can find." It was all part of the process, and they were still in the early stages. The clients told her everything they didn't like; it helped her narrow down the field. Eventually they found something that fit. But sometimes that took months.

She reached for the door handle, smiling a little when she saw a swing hanging from the sturdy branches of the nearest tree. They'd had one just like that growing up; the sisters always raced to see who could get to it first, Abby's braids flying out from behind her as she scrambled down the steps. Margo was fastest, and always stood back and let Abby go first anyway. They'd carved their names into the bottom of the seat one year, crudely etching the wood with their initials, marking what was theirs, what was special.

A sad smile pulled at her mouth. Maybe this was why she'd fallen so hard for this house. It reminded her of Mimi's house.

It reminded her of home.

*

After leaving Serenity Hills by the emergency exit (honestly, if bumping into Eddie again didn't classify as an emergency, she wasn't sure what did), Margo spent the rest of the day unpacking the random belongings she had stuffed into her suitcases in her equally harried escape from her marital home. With the items laid out on the fluffy white duvet cover, there was no denying her mental state was questionable, at best. Six pairs of underwear, an extra pair of jeans that she hadn't squeezed into since last fall (too much French onion soup at Froggy's, it would seem), a handful of mismatched socks, four bras, a stack of sweaters, and two sets of pajamas. No shoes other than the ballet flats she'd been wearing when she'd watched Ash stick his tongue down Candace's throat. She was surprised to notice that she'd packed all of her toiletries, minus a razor. But really, was there any point in shaving her legs anymore?

She sat down on the bed, considering that perk.

She'd remembered her glasses, at least, and an extra pair of contact lenses. The book that had been on her bedside table for the last three weeks. And her phone charger. She'd had the sense to bring that.

Not that her husband had bothered to call.

Telling. About as telling as carrying on behind her back.

When she was finished unpacking, she drove into town, bought laundry detergent and a bottle of wine for dinner with her sisters. Then she went back to the cottage to eat ice cream in front of the television, and tried not to think that nearly forty-eight hours had transpired since she'd left home and she was still no closer than she was when she'd left to figuring out what she was going to do next.

By the time five thirty rolled around, she had scraped the ice-cream container clean, opened another, and cleared out a bag of tortilla chips as she caught up on daytime soaps and the evening news. No missing person alerts. No heartbroken husbands pleading for the safe return of his beloved spouse.

With her stomach aching from too much junk food, Margo changed into a fresh sweater that didn't bear the spill of melted ice cream, brushed her hair into a new ponytail, and slipped back into her ballet flats. An unforgiving chill was swirling off the ocean, making her shiver as she ran to the car that was parked in the driveway. She hadn't needed a coat in Charleston at this time of year, but the weather was different in Maine. Heck, everything was different in Maine. If she stuck around much longer, she'd have to buy a coat. Have to buy a few things, actually. Or, she could just drive home, back to her sunny new construction brick Colonial on

Peach Leaf Circle, where she had a walk-in closet full of everything she would ever need.

Except a husband who loved her.

She forced her attention to the road, trying not to think about other matters right now. It would only bring her down, and she didn't want to feel down anymore. Bridget lived in an apartment near the center of town, and walking distance from Oyster Bay's shops and restaurants that lined Main Street, including the gastro pub owned and operated by Ryan Dunley, Bridget's ex and Emma's father. Margo had only been there once, when she and Ash had visited for Mom and Dad's funeral. The food had been delicious, but then, after a week of mourning and barely stopping for food, anything would have probably tasted good. Ryan had refilled their bowls with warm chowder, until they couldn't take anymore, and spicy cornbread that topped anything she'd been served down south. But that was the beginning of the end for Ryan and Bridget—the tension between them was tangible, the bickering intense, the difficult circumstances only adding to deep-rooted problems that never did get solved.

Six months later, Bridget left him. And now, out of loyalty, Margo could never go back to Dunley's for more of that cornbread. She wished she'd thought to ask for the recipe when she had the chance. She could just imagine how that would have gone over with Nadine Reynolds last Thanksgiving, when, by some twisted misunderstanding, they'd both brought cornbread to Grandmother Reynolds's house and Nadine had decided to go around the table and ask each guest whose dish they preferred.

Out of loyalty, perhaps, Ash had voted for his mother.

Loyalty. Is that what had kept her sisters from mentioning that Eddie was back in town? Or was it loyalty to Ash? Probably not. Sure, her sisters hadn't disliked Ash, not openly at least, but they'd never really warmed to him either. And it had been clear by their own romantic choices that he was far from the type they would choose.

No, Ash, being preppy and clean cut and a bit type A, was hardly their style. But then, she hadn't been his in the end, had she?

She parked the car in front of the apartment complex and walked into the courtyard clutching a bottle of wine by the neck and scolding herself to get it together before she knocked on the door. Tonight wasn't the time to burden her sisters with her marital issues, especially with Emma around. Tonight was about reconnecting and having fun, and God knew she deserved a bit of that.

She walked along the path, scanning the numbers on the doors, feeling like a bit of a heel that she didn't remember exactly where her sister's unit was, and that she had only been here a handful of times at best. She craned her neck, trying to remember if it was unit 1D or 1F, and feeling too ashamed to text and ask, when a door behind her slammed.

She turned, hoping to ask a neighbor to point her in the right direction, but the words stopped on her tongue when she saw Eddie standing in front of her.

"We meet again." His mouth curved into a smile.

Margo decided not to mention Serenity Hills, or the way she'd run off on him—something she'd love nothing more than to do again, right now. "I'm visiting my sister," she said lamely.

She stared at him, properly this time, because there was no avoiding it. The courtyard was empty and they were standing eye to eye, face to face, and God, it was nearly killing her. He'd aged since the last time she'd seen him, his features hardening, laugh lines creasing the corner of his eyes, and damn it if he wasn't more handsome than he'd been all those years ago, when he was just a boy really. She looked at his mouth, finding it nearly impossible to think she'd once kissed it, and up into his eyes, deep set and dark and just a little haunted, not much different than he'd looked that last time she'd seen him, when he kissed her forehead and whispered into her ear and lingered on her for so long she thought he might just change his mind and stay. But he couldn't stay. That part wasn't up to him. But choosing not to return was—and that was something she'd had to learn to accept.

"She's two doors down and one across. One G."

Ah, 1G. So she was way off. "I knew that."

He didn't look convinced, but said nothing to the

contrary.

"So you live here." Alone? She waited to see if he volunteered any information, but he just shrugged.

"It suits me, and I didn't want to impose on my aunt or uncle."

She nodded, still trying to understand what he was doing here at all. "What brought you back to town?"

His jaw seemed to tense at this. "Extenuating circumstances."

What the hell was that supposed to mean? He had a job, an apartment; his life, by all appearances, seemed settled. She'd just seen Lori, who had given no hint at trouble with the family.

She thought of Eddie's visit at Serenity Hills, and quickly dismissed it. He was probably following up some police business, not that she could see how anyone in that facility could cause much trouble…Well, other than Pudgie.

She opened her mouth to speak, not sure what there was to even say, even though there were so many burning questions. But Eddie jutted his chin to the street. "I should go," he said abruptly, stepping back. He gestured to the wine in her hands. "Have a nice dinner."

That was all he had to say to her? After all this time, this was it? He wanted to pretend like nothing had happened? That he had just decided to come back to town, now, not then, because of extenuating circumstances?

He wasn't her friend anymore, she realized with a

pang. Once they had told each other everything, and now he was being decidedly vague.

Margo stood there, watching him walk to his car, the ache in her chest returning as she tried to wrap her head around what had just happened, and then, before she could bother to read any more into it, she turned and went off in search of Bridget's apartment.

Eddie was trouble. He was then. He was now.

Really, she had enough trouble of her own these days. The last thing she needed was to add Eddie to the mix.

*

Emma greeted her at the door, wearing a purple iridescent princess dress, a pink plastic tiara, and a smile that boasted two missing teeth. At first glance, Margo could see that she was taller and thinner than the last time she'd visited, and the realization filled her with shame. "Auntie Margo! Look at my Halloween costume! Do you like it?" She gave a dramatic twirl, and all at once, Margo felt better.

"A fairy princess?" she guessed.

Emma stared at her. "Just a princess, silly. See? No wings?"

Ah. Of course. "Well, come here and give me a hug, princess." She swooped in to give her only niece a squeeze and then reached into her handbag to pull out the bag of chocolates she'd bought for her at the store. "You have to ask your mother first," she said, knowing how Bridget could be about things like sugar and teeth and other rules like bedtime and schedules.

"Have to ask me what?" Bridget asked, coming into the hall with Abby bouncing at her heels.

At the sight of her younger sister, Margo felt her spirit lift. "Abby!" She laughed as Abby bounded into her arms. Even at the age of twenty-eight, she was still a child at heart, and Margo half envied her for it.

Bridget surveyed them both with narrowed eyes. She didn't have the same patience when it came to Abby. "Come into the kitchen. I have wine and snacks while the lasagna's cooking. And Emma, no chocolate until dessert, please."

Emma gave a groan and Margo gave her a wink. "Hold my hand and lead the way," she said, even though the apartment was small, and the kitchen was nearly within arm's reach.

Emma deposited her bag of candy on the counter and immediately became engrossed in a coloring book at the round pedestal table that was set for four. Margo handed over the bottle of wine she'd brought with her and said, "You failed to mention that Eddie was your neighbor."

Bridget's face flushed with guilt. "I thought of saying something, but then I wasn't sure you'd still care."

Abby's green eyes were wide when Margo turned to her, brow arched. "Honestly, I didn't think you still cared about Eddie. You've been married for like…forever."

Forever. It was true. Twelve years in total had been spent with Ash, while only three short years were spent with Eddie. So why did it feel like the only person she'd ever truly been herself with was the one who knew her the shortest?

"I don't still care about Eddie," Margo said with more insistence than she felt. "But a head's up might have been nice. I just bumped into him, with no preparation." Now, that part wasn't entirely true. She did know he was in town. But that knowledge was supposed to help her avoid him, not find him.

"I'm sorry. It wasn't forefront in my mind." Bridget uncorked the bottle of wine and poured them each a glass. "Besides, I barely see him around. Our schedules don't match up."

"When did he move back?" Margo asked, hoping her tone passed for casual. She leaned against the counter and inspected a nail, but she was holding her breath, eager for information.

"It was the spring, I think." Bridget shrugged.

Margo nodded. She was burning to know more. Was he married? Kids? But what did it matter? The mystery of Eddie Boyd was solved. Closure was mostly had. She knew now how he'd turned out. Where he'd ended up. Right back in Oyster Bay.

"He's a police officer, you know," Abby offered, seemingly pleased by this fact.

"Yes, I'm aware," Margo said. "Rather ironic, isn't it?"

"Oh, are any of us really the same people we were at eighteen?" Bridget said.

"You aren't," Abby said, taking a sip of wine. "When you were eighteen you were still fun."

Margo laughed, but Bridget seemed far from amused. "Well, one of us has to be responsible around here. Between a kid, Mimi, and a job, I don't have the luxury of being fun."

"Whoa, it was just a joke," Abby said, frowning.

"Well, it's a lot to handle when I have no one to share the load." Bridget sighed and slid two glasses of wine across the breakfast bar. "Sorry, I didn't mean to snap. It's just...a lot sometimes. Lately I've been so tired I've started to wonder if I never should have left Ryan."

"Are you serious?" Margo was alarmed. Her heart was starting to race and her hand trembled as she reached for her wine glass. During their short-lived marriage, Ryan was notorious for staying out until early hours of the morning under the guise of working on payroll, when Bridget suspected he was having beers with the staff—a young crowd that was far more fun than a pregnant wife with swollen ankles. Dunley's had been a thorn in their relationship from the beginning, both financially and personally; Bridget liked to joke a little bitterly that he should have named it "The Other Woman." And when it became apparent over time that nothing was ever going to change, she'd given him an ultimatum. It hadn't resulted in the outcome she'd hoped for. Like Eddie, Ryan was far from husband material.

Ash, Ash was husband material. Or so she'd thought.

"No, I'm not serious," Bridget sighed. "I'm just worn

out is all."

"Ryan should help out more with the childcare," Abby said, lowering her voice so Emma wouldn't hear.

Bridget cocked an eyebrow. "His idea of helping out is taking Emma out for pizza and ice cream and then bringing her back all sugared up because he has to get to the restaurant. Or he'll bring her along. Let her sit at the bar and chat with whoever's tending." She shook her head and took a long drink of wine. "Sometimes I don't know what was worse: being married to him or divorced from him. At least when I was with him, there was someone to help pay the bills."

Margo took a long sip of wine, trying to curb the panic that quickened her pulse when she thought about everything that a divorce from Ash entailed. Sure, she still had access to their credit cards for now, and she had some savings from her business in their joint account. She'd get half the value of the house. But she'd need to find work and soon.

She set the glass down with a shaking hand. Was she really doing this? Making plans, uprooting her life?

She brought the glass to her lips again. What other choice did she have?

"I should have known Ryan was trouble. After all, we dated for how many years before he finally popped the question?" Bridget shook her head. "Should have gone for Jeffrey McDowell back when he asked me out. Instead he took Patricia, and look at them now!"

"But they're your best friends," Abby pointed out.

Bridget gave a sad smile. "I know. It's just easy to think of how things might have been..." She looked at Margo. "See, you don't have to worry about that, Margo. You're lucky. Eddie was bad news and he spared you, and then you ended up with the nice guy, living in a big house without a care in the world."

Without a care in the world. If Bridget only knew. Margo glanced at the table, where Emma was coloring a picture of a unicorn. Not the time to open the floodgates, and really, she didn't want to go there anyway. Not tonight.

"Ash didn't want to join you on the trip?" Abby asked.

"Oh..." And here it was. She hadn't even lied yet, and already her cheeks were getting warm and her eyes were flitting from one sister to the other. "He had business to take care of." She managed not to snort.

The answer seemed to suffice her youngest sister. Abby shrugged and reached for a cracker. "It's more fun without him anyway!"

"Abby!" Bridget cried, but for the first time in days, Margo burst out laughing.

"See?" Abby grinned. "If Ash were here, we'd all have to talk about boring pleasantries like our jobs—"

"Speaking of," Bridget cut in. "How's yours going? Still working part-time at the doctor's office?"

Abby dodged the question, as Margo suspected she would, by topping off her wine and saying, "I'm more interested in yours. Have you found a buyer for the house yet?"

The air seemed to leave the room and all smiles drooped. "I'm working on it," Bridget said tightly.

Margo couldn't hold back her feelings any longer. "Isn't there something you can do to hold on to it?"

"Did you visit Mimi today?" Bridget inquired pertly.

Margo frowned. "I did. It was…" Depressing, upsetting, eye-opening. There were so many feelings she had over the visit that she couldn't settle on just one.

"Surely now you understand. She's not capable of living on her own, much less taking care of such a big place!"

"Yes, but that's our home, too. Not just Mimi's."

Bridget's eyes widened. "So what? You're going to buy it?"

"Obviously not." She was about to say that she already had a house in South Carolina, and then stopped herself.

"I have someone coming to look at it tomorrow afternoon. We won't have another lead like this for a while. I could use some help making it shine before the showing."

Margo knew this was more of a request than an invitation. And with her background in staging and design, she couldn't exactly refuse. "What time?"

Bridget smiled. "Nine o'clock work for you? I'll come right from school drop-off."

"I can't believe I'm agreeing to this," Margo grumped, reached for a cracker, even though she had started to lose her appetite.

Bridget sighed. "Look. It's not what any of us want. But it's reality."

Truer words were never spoken. "I'm just sad to let it go, is all," she said, thinking of all the memories they'd made there. "Do you remember the time we hid in the attic and Mom couldn't find us and eventually called the police?"

Bridget burst out laughing. "I'd forgotten all about that!"

"I don't remember," Abby said, pouting.

"You were only two. We had to bribe you with candy to keep you quiet." Bridget laughed again.

"We paid for it, though. When Dad found out he grounded us for a week. Not you, Abby, of course," Margo added.

"He secretly thought it was funny, though," Bridget said. "I remember hearing him and Mom laughing downstairs after they'd ordered us to our rooms with no dinner."

At the mention of their parents, the room fell quiet, and all their smiles seemed to fade to something more wistful.

Finally, Abby broke the silence with a mischievous grin. "Enough about the house. Now can we please talk about the new guy I'm seeing?"

"Don't tell me you're still dating that homeless guy!" Bridget said.

"He's not homeless!" Abby cried. She glanced at

Margo. "Chase lives in his van. And it's only temporary."

Bridget cocked an eyebrow. "Homeless."

Margo was fascinated. "Where does he shower?"

Abby inspected her nails. "Oh, down at the beach house."

Margo laughed. "Then he is homeless."

Bridget pursed her lips. "Yep."

"He's not—" But now Abby was laughing too. "But he's so cute! And he plays the guitar. He's in a band," she said dreamily.

Bridget grabbed two potholders from a drawer and opened the oven. "Abby, he dumpster dives," she said flatly, and Margo almost choked on her wine.

"Only for the good stuff! You know The Lantern and the hotel throw out their catch every day! Whatever didn't sell. Out it goes!"

Bridget caught Margo's eyes and sputtered loudly, nearing dropping the lasagna dish in her hand as she erupted into laughter.

"What's so funny? What's so funny?" Emma asked, looking up from her coloring book.

"Oh, honey. It's just sister talk," Margo said, and for the first time in days felt something in her heart other than sadness. Sister talk. She'd gone too long without it.

By the time Margo left, her ribs ached from laughing so hard and she'd cried off most of her mascara. She glanced around the courtyard for any sign of Eddie and hurried to unlock her car. Leaning her head back against the seat, she sighed with content.

Abby was right. The night had been more fun without Ash. And what did that say?

Chapter Five

Margo woke at eight the next morning to sunlight pouring through the curtains. The room was completely still, and she straightened out her legs, luxuriating in the stretch, and then rolled over, silently scolding herself when she saw the perfectly smooth pillow and duvet on the left side of the bad.

Force of habit, she supposed. Somehow, subconsciously, she was still playing wife. Still following the rules of their marriage, one where she slept on the right side of the bed and never crossed the imaginary line that had somehow formed over time.

It had been a long time since she'd rolled over, reached for him. It wasn't an active decision, more like a gradual process. They had known each other so long, been together since she was twenty and he was twenty-two.

And even at the beginning theirs was a relationship based more on comfort than on passion. She'd thought that was enough.

But maybe…maybe Ash hadn't. Maybe Ash had been looking for something more. Just not with her.

She squeezed her eyes shut against the pull in her chest and then flung them open again. She had promised her sister she would help her today and that made her accountable, for getting up, for acting like an adult, for pretending like her life wasn't falling to pieces around her. She tossed the bedding back, vowing to do better tonight, to sleep right in the center of the bed, stretch out diagonally, claim her newfound freedom. She stood up, pulled on the same pair of jeans she'd worn yesterday and a fresh sweater, deciding to hold off on a shower until after she'd come back from the house.

When she finished securing her hair into a ponytail, she made a cup of coffee and gulped it down with two slices of toast and wild blueberry preserves, closing her eyes at the perfection of the taste that could only be found in her home state.

Bridget couldn't meet her until nine, after she'd seen Emma off to school. Eager to get moving before her thoughts spun her into a dark place, Margo grabbed her keys and drove into town, this time with a new destination in mind.

It might be early, but that's when her mother's brother Chip met the fish monger each morning, as he had for as long as she could remember.

His restaurant, The Lantern, was at the edge of town, on the way toward the marina, where traffic slowed but never enough to keep the line from creeping out the door at peak hours. No one made crab cakes like Chip, or lobster rolls, for that matter either.

She spotted Chip standing outside near the back door as she pulled the car to a stop in front of the restaurant. Crates were at his feet, no doubt the fresh catch of the day, and she hurried over the gravel pathway to stop him before he could disappear into the kitchen.

"Chip!" She never bothered with the Uncle bit, and he'd preferred it that way. Said it made him feel old, even if he was their mother's older brother by three years.

Chip shielded his eyes from the sun with a hand and then broke out into a smile. "Margo? Well aren't you a sight!" He was grinning as she approached. "I'd tell you to give me a hug, but I've been gutting fish all morning."

"Like that could stop me," Margo said, leaning in to give him a squeeze. She closed her eyes, daring to let herself be held, finding it strange how you could go for years without seeing someone and feel like no time had ever passed at all, other than the sensation that you'd missed that person, and more than you'd known.

"I've been away too long," she said with regret. She was happy for the sunglasses that shielded the tears in her eyes. She loved Chip, loved his burly exterior and his soft heart. Loved the boom of his laughter and the sight of his smile and the way he always told stories of her mother, and that he was the only one who could do that anymore.

He brushed a hand through the air. "Ah, you're busy. A married woman. My own girls rarely come back anymore." His blue eyes turned a little cloudy and he opened another crate, tossing the lid to the side.

Hannah had gone to live with her mother in San Francisco shortly after college, something that Chip would never admit had hurt him greatly, even if a part of him understood her need. Chip had married and divorced soon after his second daughter was born—a break-up that hadn't been his choice and which had left him alone with two little girls to care for. He'd had to learn to brush and braid hair and paint nails, and eventually deal with all the teenage drama that no one could avoid. Margo's mother had always hoped Chip would remarry, but he'd been burned, even if he was too tough to ever say so.

"How long are you staying in town?"

"Undecided," Margo said.

"Ash with you?" Chip looked confused.

Margo shrugged her shoulders, knowing she could make up an excuse, but knowing with Chip, she didn't need to. "Nope."

Chip eyeing her critically. "Everything okay, Mags?" He was the only person who called her that, and she loved him for it. "I promised my sister I'd look after you girls, you know. If anything ever…Well, you know." He frowned, looked back at the lobster in his hand, wrestled with its claw a bit.

At the mention of her mother, Margo's throat grew

tight. "Everything will be okay," she said with more confidence than she felt. "I'm just working through some things. Came home to clear my head."

"Oyster Bay is good for that. These are your roots. If you can't figure things out here, where can you?"

She nodded thoughtfully. So far, she wasn't thinking any clearer than she had when she'd first decided to come back. Less clearly, in fact, thanks to Eddie. "I hope you're right."

Chip gave a single nod and set the lobster back in the crate. "Well, I can't say I've had much success when it comes to matters of the heart, but if you ever feel like talking, you know where to find me."

"That's sort of why I stopped by," she said, grinning apologetically. "Sorry it wasn't just for a social call."

"What's up?" Chip frowned.

"I'm sure you know about my grandmother."

Chip sighed. "I do. I'm sorry. I know you were close."

Were close. Past tense. They had been close, as close as mother and daughter for a while, but then somehow it had slipped away. Margo had gotten busy. Let the routine of things like work and grocery shopping and deciding how to spend a free Saturday afternoon interfere with their relationship. She didn't call every week. Sometimes, she didn't even call every month.

"I feel terrible," she said, her voice cracking. She pulled in a shaky breath, wiped a single hot tear from her eye before it could fall. "I should have reached out more."

"You visited when you could. It's not like you live an hour away. This is life, Margo. You have a husband and a job and responsibilities, too. Don't be so hard on yourself."

She highly doubted Bridget would see it that way. "Still. If I'd known how bad things were, I would have come back for a visit."

Chip gave her a sad smile. "I know it's hard to believe, but it wouldn't have changed the outcome. Your grandmother's where she needs to be. She's lived a good life."

Margo sniffed. "I know you're right."

"What was that?" A mischievous grin lifted Chip's mouth as he leaned forward, dramatically cupping his ear. "Think you can say that in front of one of my girls sometime?"

"How are Evie and Hannah?" she asked, feeling better.

"Ah, Evie's still in Boston, finishing up her degree, and Hannah…Well, you know Hannah. I got a postcard from Argentina last week. Seems she's photographing some wildlife there."

"She always was a free spirit."

"Free as a bird," Chip's smile waned. "I never could keep her down. Much as I'd love to, it wouldn't be fair."

"Well, send them my love," Margo said, taking a step back. The smell of fish was strong and she had the distinct feeling it was starting to wear off on her. "I should go. I promised Bridget that I'd help her with the house today."

"Stop by one night for dinner. I'll make you your favorite."

"Crab cakes?" Now that was more like it.

Chip winked. "You know it."

"I'll come in tomorrow night. Love you, Uncle Chip," she said. She hesitated, noticing the salmon he held in his hands, and then thought, to hell with it and leaned in for one more hug. She'd lost enough people in her life already. She could stand to hold the ones she still had a little tighter.

"Love you, Mags. And remember," he said, wagging his finger at her as she walked to the car. "Always here if you need me. Always."

"Thanks," she said. "I might take you up on that."

*

The driveway to the house was empty when Margo pulled up ten minutes later. She checked her watch; it wasn't like Bridget to be late.

Still, a part of her was happy to have the house to herself for a bit. She pushed back the nagging feeling that it could be for the last time.

The hydrangeas that lined the wraparound porch had finished their bloom for the year, their leaves had already fallen off, leaving nothing but a series of spiky branches poking from the ground. Margo had loved those flowers, looked forward to them every July, when they popped up, bursting with big round balls in shades of blue periwinkle and lavender. She'd pick big bunches and fill vases all over the house, even loving them still when the color had faded to shades of green.

Would she really never see them at their peak again? Back in Charleston, she had planted a bush, but it didn't take, no matter how much she tended to it. Life was like that, she supposed. Sometimes the harder you had to work at something, the more difficult it became to hold onto it. Like the universe was trying to tell you something.

Had it been that way with Ash? At times, she thought. If she was being honest with herself.

Someone had filled the front planters with bright orange mums—Bridget, most likely. Margo was no dummy. It would be tough to sell a place in Oyster Bay in the winter, when the seas were rough and the winds were bitter. Spring and summer was when this old house shone the brightest. And by then...by then it would probably belong to someone else. Would they love it has much as the Harpers had? Would they explore the attic and the basement and the secret door hidden behind the bookshelf in the living room that didn't lead to anywhere in particular, just another closet? Would they climb on the rocks that met the sand, pretending they were mermaids, or castaways on a deserted island? Would they lie in bed at night with the window cracked so they could hear the waves rolling, and wake to the sound of the gulls flying and swooping overhead? And would they gather in the front room on Christmas Eve, listening to the fire crackle, not caring that the snow was piling up outside or that they'd eventually have to get around to shoveling the front path, almost not wanting Christmas to come because the magic would be over?

Margo walked around to the back of the house and tried the doors to the kitchen, even though she knew they would be locked just as they had been yesterday. She craned her neck, looking up at the far right corner of the house where her bedroom was located, and whose window was always unlocked, at least when she'd lived here. She chewed her lip and ran her gaze over the white rose trellis that climbed the side of the house.

Huh. She stepped off the porch and wandered over to it. Gave it a tentative shake, both pleased and surprised that it barely moved. It had always been sturdy, nailed deep into the wood siding, but she wasn't exactly as svelte as she'd been fifteen years ago, either. Tentatively, she set her foot in one of the holes, then the next, gaining confidence as she took her time moving up the trellis, careful not to look down.

She was out of breath by the time she stepped onto the roof of the first-floor sunroom, her bedroom window now just walking distance from where she stood. She pressed her hands against the glass, pushing upward, grinning when it moved an inch. Frowning when it stopped there.

What the heck? She pushed harder, peering through

the sunlight reflecting off the window. Something was blocking it from opening farther. Someone had attached something to the frame.

She was still pondering this minutes later when the beep of a siren broke the silence, as sudden and jolting as the snapping of a branch. She froze, her heart beginning to pound when the sound drew closer. A car door slammed shut and a few moments later, Eddie emerged around the corner of the house.

Well, crap.

She crouched down, trying to hide behind the branches of the old oak tree, but its leaves had already started to scatter to the ground, crunching under Eddie's feet as he looked up and came to an abrupt halt.

"Well, well." A mischievous grin quirked his mouth.

"Hello," Margo mustered, not sure if she should stand, but feeling foolish hiding in the branches. She fiddled with a leaf, tried to take on the air of looking busy while she racked her brain for a reasonable explanation.

She glanced down. He stood, set his hands on his hips, signaling he wasn't going anywhere any time soon. Pity that.

"Everything okay here?" God, did his voice have to be so warm and husky and familiar?

"Of course!" She sniffed, reached over and plucked a leaf from the branch, considering her options.

"We received a call from the home security company," Eddie continued. "Seems that someone tripped the alarm."

"Oh?" She felt her cheeks flush. "Well, that was a false alarm. It was only me."

"And what were you doing?" Eddie tipped his head, waiting oh so patiently.

"I was trying to get into my bedroom," she said, realizing how pathetic that sounded.

"And why didn't you just use the door?"

She stared at him. "Because I don't have a key."

He nodded, and for a minute she thought he might turn, go back to his car, and leave. Instead he said, "And are you the owner of this house?"

Oh, for crying out loud! He knew the answer to every question he was asking, but he was asking them all the same. To do his job, to cover his butt. Or to mess with her.

He stared at her until her stomach dropped from more than the way his hazel eyes caught the light.

"Well, no, not technically." She gave a nervous laugh. "Are you being serious?"

He raised his eyebrows, took his sweet time in shifting the weight on his feet, and then shook his head. "*Technically*, you are breaking and entering. And trespassing. But seeing as I don't think your grandmother would press charges against you, I'll let you off with a warning."

She blinked. A warning? Another warning, *technically*, since they were speaking in technicalities now.

"A warning," she repeated, looking down at him. As if

the curl of his mouth and the spark in his eyes wasn't warning enough.

"You know how dangerous it is to climb up that lattice?" He walked over, grabbed hold of it, and gave it a little shake.

"Never stopped me before," Margo replied, wishing she hadn't gone there, but seeing no other handy defense.

Eddie's laugh was thick and low, but it faded out to a long silence. He swept his hand through his hair, looked out to the sea. "No, I suppose it didn't. But we were reckless, then."

Correction: *He* was reckless. He liked thrills, and he couldn't control his temper, even when she held him back, told him to ignore the stuff the kids at school said, told him that it didn't matter. She opened her mouth to say just that and then stopped herself. Maybe he was right, maybe she had been reckless, too. Reckless enough to fall for the bad boy, to sneak out her bedroom window when her parents were already asleep for the night and Mimi was in the den, watching game shows late into the night and sipping tea, not to be disturbed. Reckless enough to climb off a roof, to hop on the back of a motorcycle, to disappear into the night. Reckless enough to believe Eddie when he told her that he loved her, that they'd have a life together someday, that he'd be back for her.

Reckless enough to go and marry the first nice guy who came along, without looking too close.

"Well, you're not going to get down the way you came

up," Eddie finally said.

Margo looked down at the ground. It suddenly seemed a lot farther than it ever had before. "No, I suppose not." She studied the tree limbs and shivered at the wind blowing in off the water. She caught Eddie's stare, sensing the glimmer that passed through his eyes.

"I'm happy to call the fire department," he said evenly. "They've got a nice tall ladder that can get you down in no time. Of course, it's usually reserved for rescuing cats, but I'm sure they'd be willing to make an exception this once."

Margo narrowed her eyes. "Very funny."

Eddie just shrugged and turned to walk away. "Suit yourself. I'm sure you've thought this through."

Margo grit her teeth. "There might be a ladder in the shed."

He stopped walking. His mouth twitched when he looked up at her. "If the shed's unlocked."

Right. Margo was breathing more heavily now.

"I'll check," Eddie said, and walked around to the side of the house, whistling as he went.

Margo closed her eyes and dared to imagine this was all a dream. That she was back in Charleston, in her house, secure in the comfort that later that evening her husband would come home from work, they'd eat dinner, briefly exchanging the details of their day, and then separate for the night—her to read, him to watch the news—before retiring to bed where she slept on her side and he on his and where there was no good night kiss. No passion. No drama. No excitement. And nothing to fear.

She'd been comfortable, she realized, but had she really been happy?

Now wasn't the time to soul search, she decided. Now was the time to get off this damn roof before Eddie could play knight in shining armor. A role he wholly didn't deserve.

She rolled over onto her stomach, blindly jostled her ballet flat into the trellis, crept her other leg a little lower as she pressed her hands against the shingles of the roof and...lost her nerve.

The whistling grew louder, the song replaced with something that sounded an awful lot like a cat call.

Refusing to think of how unflattering she looked, she decided to shed all dignity and accept her situation. It beat breaking a leg. "Please tell me you found the ladder."

He waited a beat. "I found the ladder."

Well, thank God for small miracles. She waited until he'd propped the ladder against the sunroom and then shimmied over to it, carefully easing her way down, until her feet were on steady ground. She turned, setting her jaw as she knew she had to thank him, and startled when she realized how close he was standing.

She swallowed hard, tried not to look too closely at the jaw or those lips or those eyes. He reached up, muttering something as he brought a hand to her face. Her heart sped up, wondering what he was doing, where he was going with this. If he'd had a change of heart, now, after all this time. His hand brushed her ear, curled around her neck, and she stiffened in awareness, waiting, wondering.

"There," he said, grinning. "You had a leaf stuck in your ponytail." He held up the evidence, then released it to blow in the breeze.

Of course. As if he were about to…Oh, she didn't know what she thought he was about to do. Or what she'd have done if he had.

Eddie sniffed the air, his nose wrinkling. "What is that smell?"

Margo's pulse flickered. She thought of hugging Chip. The salmon. The lobster. "I don't smell anything."

His brow pinched, but he dropped the subject.

"You okay?" he asked, and his voice was so low and soft that for a moment she wondered if he knew. About her and Ash. About Candy. About the kiss. About every tear she'd ever cried for him, her husband, for the way life hadn't turned out the way it was supposed to. "No scrapes or cuts?"

Of course. He was probably one step away from offering to call an ambulance. "I'm fine," she said, brushing past him and marching around to the front of the house where Bridget's car was pulling into the driveway.

She wasn't fine. But he didn't need to know that. Besides, she'd be fine. Somehow.

Chapter Six

Eddie was barely out of the driveway when his phone rang. Not his work phone. His personal phone. His chest tightened as he pulled to a stop on the side of the road, bracing himself for whatever news was about to come. Few people had access to this number, and those that did had no good reason for calling.

He pulled the device from his pocket and looked at the screen, frowning when he saw the Philly area code. His mind went to a dozen places all at once, trying to place the source. He hadn't spoken to his old sponsor since about a month after he'd moved back to Oyster Bay and established himself in a support group twenty minutes west, where he could still be anonymous. Besides, he knew Josh's number. Had it stored. It could be Jesse, the kid he'd been trying to help for the last two years, ever since he picked him up for the third time for petty theft that wouldn't be petty much longer with the pattern he had going. Jesse didn't have a father, and his mother was checked out, more focused on keeping her new boyfriend happy than taking care of her two sons—a scenario Eddie understood more than the kid would ever know. So, Eddie struck a deal. If Jesse went to school every day, stopped stealing from the store on the corner, and kept his grades up, Eddie would help him get into college. For a while, the arrangement stuck, until last year when Jesse fell in with a worse crowd than before, and disappeared again. Eddie had left Philadelphia without knowing where the boy was, or if he was okay, and with the sinking feeling that he hadn't done enough, that he'd somehow failed.

The phone rang again, possibly for the last time before voicemail kicked in. Without giving any more thought, he tapped the screen, put the phone to his ear, and held his breath.

"Eddie Boyd," he said, his voice tight in his throat.

"Eddie!"

Oh, thank God. It was Mick O'Grady—he'd recognize his old partner's voice anywhere. How many times had it been just the two of them in the squad car, cruising the streets, stopping for an early lunch or a late dinner, refilling their coffee cups and trying to keep things light despite some of the things they saw in the day.

"You get a new number?" he asked, wondering why it

wasn't stored in his list.

"A new job," Mick clarified. "They moved me over to narcotics."

Eddie gave a long whistle. "That's quite a promotion."

"I guess you could say that," Mick said, and Eddie grinned. That was Mick. Always humble.

"What do they have you doing over there? More than pushing paper, I imagine." Mick had been a star on the force for the last three years, and Eddie knew when an opportunity came along that Mick would be tapped for it. Not that Mick was calling to boast. No, he must have had another reason to call.

Sure enough, Mick explained his position in a vague, roundabout way, without ever coming out and saying he was now heading up the division. "We need a strong team," he finally said. "Which is why I'm hoping you'll come back. Be my right-hand man, like before."

A position at the top of a division was more than Eddie had ever imagined, and certainly more exciting than fetching kitties out of trees or helping women down from roofs. He swallowed hard, trying not to think of Margo's long legs and bright green eyes, the determined defiance that shone through them.

He shook that feeling off. Margo was a married woman. She wasn't sticking around town for long. At best she'd give him a chance to explain, to try to set their past right. But there was no future with Margo.

Maybe, he thought sadly, there never had been.

"It's a chance to make a difference," Mick said.

Eddie nodded, even though Mick couldn't see. He knew, more than Mick could ever understand. It was why he'd become a cop to begin with, why he dedicated his life to something better.

But there was another part of his life here in Oyster Bay, a reason he'd come back—a reason that Mick didn't know about. That no one other than his aunt and uncle were aware of. The question was, where was he needed most?

"Give me a few days to think about it?" he finally said.

"Of course," Mick said, "but don't take too long. And please say yes," he laughed, but Eddie suspected he was only half-joking. "I'll call you next Friday."

A week from now. Eddie hung up the phone and sat in the car for a long time, thinking of where he'd been and how far he'd come, and wondering just how to avoid slipping back into that place he'd run from—the angry kid with something to prove.

He wasn't angry anymore, not really. Time had healed most wounds, as had experience, but there were some things, some parts of his past and himself that would always stay with him. For the good and the bad.

*

"What was Eddie doing here?" Bridget asked as she punched the code into the lock box and retrieved the key.

"Just patrolling the area," Margo said vaguely. No need to tell her sister she'd been climbing the lattice. Knowing

Bridget, she'd lose her temper and accuse Margo of trying to sabotage the sale of the property by damaging the structure.

"Well, that's nice of him," Bridget said instead. "He knows the house is vacant." She paused, glancing sideling at Margo. "And that was it? Nothing more?"

"Of course not!" Margo said, raising her chin. "Eddie's just a guy I dated when I was a kid." She was about to say that she was a married woman now and stopped herself. She didn't want to get into another conversation about Ash. Their time was limited if they wanted to get the work done before the client showed up.

"If you say so," Bridget sighed and pushed open the door.

Margo opened her mouth to argue, but her words fell flat when the door swung open. She couldn't help it. The moment they stepped into the large hallway lined with family photos, tears filled her eyes. She walked into the front sitting room, still furnished with the same well-loved and well-worn armchairs grouped around the fireplace. The piano was nestled in the bay window; it probably hadn't been touched since last Christmas. The holidays were always a cheerful time in this house. Full of laughter and music and trays of cookies.

She tapped a few keys on the piano—sure enough, it needed tuning—and then crossed the room to the French doors that led into the dining room, with its heavy cherry wood furniture and buffet filled with hand-painted china, passed down through generations.

Who would get it all, she wondered now, suddenly hoping it would be her. In fairness, they should divide the set. But Abby wouldn't take care of it, and it would be a shame to scatter the pieces amongst them.

She looked at her sister, realizing that it was Bridget who should have the dishes. She was the only one of them with a daughter to pass them onto someday. She and Ash had talked about children early on in their marriage, but then they'd both gotten busy with their careers, and other things, it would seem...

Now the loss hit her hard. There was no longer a someday. No longer the possibility of a real family of her own. It wasn't just Ash she was losing. Or the life they'd built. It was the life she'd dreamed of that was now gone too.

Bridget's frown seemed to mirror her own. "It's not easy coming back here, I know." She huffed out a breath, but all Margo could do was shake her head.

It wasn't easy. It wasn't easy at all. But not for the reasons Bridget suspected. Standing in these rooms with someone else's belongings and furniture and treasures, filled her with a sense of longing more than nostalgia. Yes, it was her childhood home, where she'd grown from a baby to an adult of eighteen, ready to flee the nest. But it wasn't her home. Not really.

Her home was a brick Colonial with a bright white kitchen and a center island where she always kept the fruit bowl filled with Granny Smith apples, because the shade of green was so perky. Her home was the house with the cozy living room with the built-in bookcases surrounding the brick fireplace and the mirror that hung above it, which she'd spent ten months shopping for, eager to make sure it was just right. When she opened the pantry, all of her favorite foods were there, and when she climbed into bed at night, it was under the sheets she had selected, not too thin, not too thick.

They'd chosen the house for the yard—big and square with just the right amount of shade. Never much of a green thumb, Margo had painfully researched flowers, visiting nurseries every few days, learning about which varieties needed sun over shade, which were hardier to the climate. When her first rose bush bloomed, she'd taken a photo of it.

Every single thing in that house had been chosen with care, exactly to her taste and comfort. And now...now she wasn't sure she could ever go home again. Or if she even wanted to.

"I've cleared out most of Mimi's favorite things," Bridget was saying. "But I've left everything in its place and, well..." The sisters exchanged a knowing look. "It needs some freshening up. And I want it to feel inviting."

"I wish I had access to my prop closet right now," Margo sighed. She'd been asked to stage homes before, and she'd started stashing staples like candlesticks and vases and throw pillows for when the need arose. This house was beautiful, but Bridget was right, it needed a little help if they were going to get top dollar for it.

Her jaw set at that thought. Best not to think about it now.

Instead, she walked into the kitchen, which was tidy, but bare, and more dated than it ever felt when it was filled with family, gathered around the center island. The butcher block counters showed signs of wear and the fixtures needed updating, but there wasn't time for any of that now. "Let's get some flowers for the table," she said, thinking of quick fixes to brighten the space. "Some for the dining room, too." She scanned the room, deciding to clear away the ceramic canisters near the range to make the space look bigger. "What time is the showing?"

"Two," Bridget said.

That wouldn't leave much opportunity. "Let's add another bouquet on the island. Sunflowers would be nice."

Bridget nodded. "I can pick some up in town and be back in twenty minutes."

They went upstairs next, to the master bedroom, which was still an homage to Mimi's married days. When Margo's parents had moved in with her, they'd taken the suite at the far back of the house instead, with the girls' rooms scattered between, on various sides of the long hallway. Mimi's wedding quilt covered the bed, its navy and red tones darkening the room. Without allowing room for sentiment, Margo folded it and handed it to Bridget. "Mimi should have this with her anyway, and we need to make this space feel more open and airy."

"Oh!" Bridget wriggled her nose as she took the quilt from Margo's arms. "That stench!" She sniffed the blanket as Margo's cheeks flamed. "I swear I cleaned out the fridge when Mimi moved. Do you smell that?"

Margo swallowed hard. "Actually, that might be me."

"You?" Bridget's eyes widened in surprise, but she started to laugh.

"I went down to The Lantern to see Chip this morning. He was unloading his fresh catch."

"Well, take it off, please! And before I leave, remind me that I have a coat for you in my trunk. Just don't you dare put it on until you've showered!" Bridget set the quilt in the oak trunk at the foot of the bed and closed the lid. "I'll find another quilt in the attic and hope it hasn't been eaten by moths."

Margo did as she was told and went into her childhood bedroom, which had been reduced over the years to a guest room, aside from a few old items in the closet and her floral bedding set. She changed into an old T-shirt she pulled from a hanger, frowning at how snug it fit, and shivered at the draft. Sure enough, the window was still open a crack. She muttered to herself as she crossed the room and closed it.

She didn't need any more reminders of that embarrassing run-in with Eddie.

Really, she didn't need any reminders of Eddie at all.

Chapter Seven

Bridget stood on the front porch of her childhood home, heart thumping nearly as fast as it had the first time Ryan had pulled up in his dad's navy blue sedan to pick her up for dinner. It was strange to think of how young they'd been then. How exciting each interaction had been. How she'd hung on his every word, delighted in his laugh, shivered at the slightest touch.

My, how much had changed.

Sometimes she wondered, looking back, what she would have done if she knew what she did now. Would she still have married him? The answer was, of course, yes. Ryan had given her Emma—and all the heartache and hardship that followed was worth it for that one, perfect gift.

Still, it would be nice if their life was a bit more settled.

She couldn't help but want her daughter to have all the comfort she'd been given growing up right here, in this old house, that had been in their family for generations. She'd taken for granted that she could wake to the sound of waves crashing on the rocks as she came down the stairs on Sunday mornings to sit at the old farmhouse table in the kitchen, a stack of pancakes being passed around, everyone and everything she loved and needed right beside her.

But now, most of those people were gone in some way or another. Margo lived across the country, Abby was in her own world half the time, Mimi was a ghost of the person she'd once been, and their parents...She blinked quickly, desperate to compose herself. Her parents hadn't lived to see what a mess her life had become, and she was glad for that. And they hadn't lived to see the day that she would sell this house, and she was grateful for that, even if it still broke her heart, now, after all these years, to think that they were gone and never coming back.

But she had Emma. Her sweet, funny little girl who wrote her letters and drew her pictures and was always happy to offer a hug. And that was all she needed now.

And this, she told herself firmly, was why she would sell this house. And focus on her future. Not her past. Each house she sold meant more opportunities for her daughter. And this was her biggest listing ever.

She cleared her throat, waiting for the blur in her eyes to evaporate, and straightened her shoulders as a black convertible drew closer on the gravel drive. A flutter of panic swam through her stomach, but there was no time to dwell on that now. Game face. Go time. This was her chance for a better future. For all of them.

The door opened and out stepped a man. Tall, lean, in dark jeans and a quarter-zip charcoal grey sweater. He grinned when he saw her and this time her stomach flipped from something much worse than panic. If she didn't know better, she might say it was from plain and simple desire.

"Mr. Fowler, I presume?" Her voice was high and her palms were sweating. As discreetly as possible, she brushed her right hand against her pant leg before extending it.

Lordy, he was even cuter up close, with warm brown eyes that crinkled at the corners when he smiled.

"Welcome to Oyster Bay." *Stay professional, Bridget. Eye on the prize.*

"It's a charming town you have here," he said.

"It is, it certainly is." Not exactly witty, but she couldn't think clearly from the strength of his grip. How long had it been since a man—make that an attractive man—had touched her?

His eyes took on a slightly puzzled look, as if reading her mind. Crap. She was still holding his hand, much longer than necessary.

Quickly, she dropped it. "How was the drive up?"

"Light traffic, can't complain." He stuffed his hands into his pockets and leaned back on his heels to look up at the house behind her. "The photos didn't do this place justice."

"I hope that's a good thing."

"A very good thing," he said, locking her eyes as a wide grin took over his face.

She smiled back, felt her eyelashes flutter in a way she hadn't been sure they could anymore, and...giggled.

Uh-oh.

"Well." She cleared her throat, feeling her cheeks heat as she turned to the door, which was already unlocked. "Let's hope you like the inside as much you like the outside."

"I'm sure it won't be a problem," he said, and Bridget frowned as she opened the door wide. It was an odd comment. Still, she wouldn't read into it. This was a beautiful, well-loved house on the waterfront. Of course there wouldn't be a problem.

She stepped back to let him pass, but he held out his hand and said, "Ladies first."

And she might have swooned. There was that grin again. Her sweaty palms were back. Couldn't he just stop...smiling for a minute? Or better yet, couldn't she? She didn't smile. Not like this, at least. She smiled with her daughter, or when Jeffrey said something funny at work, but other than that...She was serious, Abby had always accused. No fun, Ryan had claimed. What neither of them understood was that someone had to be the responsible one.

But now she felt downright giddy. Misplaced

excitement, she told herself firmly. She'd been anticipating this meeting for two weeks, since the email first popped up from the man standing right here, claiming he saw her listing on the MLS and wanted to come to Maine for a look. She'd been anticipating this meeting with every sense: dread, fear, with more emotions than she could dare to process. She'd try to check each one, keep herself focused and professional, but now she was starting to unravel, and that wouldn't do.

She briskly walked by him and led him straight into the front living room, glancing at the piano in the corner, which Margo had insisted on propping open, even though the thing was painfully out of tune. Last Christmas, Emma had begged her for lessons and Bridget had spent most of December researching her options, thinking she could budget for it if Ryan went in on the gift with her. But then Mimi had taken a turn for the worse, leaving on the burner on the gas range, which Bridget luckily discovered when she stopped by to drop off dinner one night, and Bridget knew it was time to move her into Serenity Hills. The piano would never fit in her apartment, or Ryan's, and so all talk of lessons had been shelved for now.

She pushed back that never-ending guilt that she wasn't giving her daughter the life she deserved, and stole another glance at her client.

"This is a large room," he observed.

"It is." She nodded. She was about to refer him to the dimensions on the listing sheet and realized with horror she had never handed him one. Good grief. Flustered, she fumbled in her handbag for her folder and quickly handed him the information. "I've always considered the fireplace in this room to be the prettiest in the house," she said, walking over to the mantle. Until this morning, it had been lined with framed photos, but Margo had cleared those away, anchoring the mirror by two pillar candles she'd repurposed from the dining room instead. "There are three other fireplaces," she said, turning.

But Ian Fowler wasn't admiring the craftsmanship of the millwork from which red and green stockings hung every December, or the ornate iron grate that Bridget once feared would be too heavy for Santa to maneuver. He was rubbing his jaw, eyes scanning the room, as if he were making some mental calculation.

Furniture placement, Bridget thought, her heart skipping a beat. A good sign, technically.

Ian walked over to the far wall and pounded it with the side of his fist.

"The walls are plaster," she said, frowning slightly.

He looked at the ceiling, following the wall to the where it met its end. "Might be able to open this up."

"What?"

The alarm in her voice caused him to look at her sharply. "I don't think it's a support wall."

She didn't know what it was, other than the wall that housed the oil painting her grandfather had painted for

Mimi on their twentieth wedding anniversary. A painting that should probably be with her in the nursing home, but which fit so perfectly into this room, she couldn't bear to take it down just yet.

"It would certainly open up the space, bring in more light," he was saying.

Bridget's chest felt heavy. She supposed he was right.

She swallowed hard and willed herself not to give away her personal feelings. The man did not need to know that this was her childhood home. It was, legally speaking, her grandmother's home. Professionally, none of that should even matter. She was commissioned to sell it, and sell it was what she would do. If not to Ian Fowler, then to somebody else. For everyone's sakes, things would proceed smoother if she treated this listing as impartially as any other. It was a product, and she was going to move it.

"I love the windows," Ian said, and Bridget couldn't help but beam with pride.

"Original to the home, but very well maintained. Double paned," she added. "The insulation here is very strong."

Ian nodded. "Structure is very important to me. That and the view, of course."

Of course. It was of no surprise that the land would be the selling point, but as Bridget led Ian through the dining room, curiosity got the better of her. This was a large house with six bedrooms and a full third floor with loads of potential. What did this man plan to do with so much space?

She glanced at his left hand. No ring.

And shame on her for being so pleased by that discovery.

She continued the tour into the kitchen, noting that Ian made no comment about the room. Bridget took that as a good thing, or an indication that as a bachelor, he might prefer takeout to cooking. She unlocked the French doors and led him out onto the back porch, with an expansive view of the grass that sloped down to the shoreline.

"This is a perfect backyard for a wedding," he surprised her by saying.

At that, Bridget, who had been leading the way down the stairs to the lawn, missed the next step and managed not to fall flat on her back only by the quick reaction of Ian, whose sturdy hands were on her back and arm, righting her before the blood could even rush to her cheeks. But rush it did. She let out a nervous laugh, and muttered her thanks, feeling the heat of mortification spread down her neck.

Ian just gave her a pleasant smile in return, and for a moment she dared to imagine the two of them standing right here, at the base of the stairs, their friends and family gathered on the lawn, where a huge white tent would be set up for their reception. Her dress would be long and elegant, and the music would be low enough to still make out the rhythm of the waves in the distance, and he'd hold out his hand and crack that smile and they'd take their first dance to the delight of everyone who had come to witness their happy day.

A wedding. She hadn't just imagined that he'd said that, had she? Was he…flirting with her?

"I'd like to take some pictures, if that's all right with you." He pulled out his phone.

"Of course." She stepped back, while he took some shots of the back of the house.

A wedding. Hadn't she always dreamed of that? A wedding right here in her own backyard? The sisters had all shared in that dream in their own unique way, imagining the flowers they'd chose (tulips for Margo, roses for Bridget, and not surprisingly, wildflowers for Abby). Instead, Bridget had eloped, Margo had been roped into the wedding of her mother-in-law's wishes, and Abby…Abby seemed to have no interest in settling down.

That left Emma. And now Emma would never have the opportunity the rest of them had squandered.

"Should we see the rest of the house?" she asked. They hadn't even been upstairs yet, and she was eager to get back inside, alone with this man. It might not even be so bad if he bought it. A single, attractive man of appropriate age who was clearly financially secure and successful and who was talking about a future and weddings. Why, if she played her cards straight, this house might just stay in the family after all!

"Let me just take a few more of the view," he said, snapping another photo. He gave her a lopsided grin and oh, if her stomach didn't roll over. "I promised my fiancée I'd send these to her."

Fiancée.

Bridget's smile tightened as she turned to go up the porch steps, her tread slow. She'd dared to hope, she realized. Something she hadn't done in a long, long time.

Something she'd be careful not to do again.

Chapter Eight

The Harper family had been coming to The Lantern ever since Uncle Chip opened the place, back when Margo's parents were newlyweds. The family had celebrated everything here: lobster with garlic mashed potatoes for birthdays; clam chowder with biscuits for New Year's Day lunch; and ice cream sundaes for good grades or other special events like, say, Margo's disastrous performance in the school talent show.

When their parents had died, the sisters agreed it was fitting for the reception to be held in the restaurant rather than at home, and Chip closed the business for the day, made his sister's favorite dishes, and half the town had stopped by and hugged them and cried with them, and as awful as that day had been, Margo knew it could have been worse. She had her friends and family surrounding her, sharing in her grief. It wasn't until she went home to her house in Charleston that the sorrow hit her, and there was no one to talk to, no one who could understand. Ash had tried, but he didn't understand. He hadn't known her parents, hadn't been a part of their memories, hadn't shared in so much of her life.

"I still don't see why I couldn't bring Pudgie," Mimi grumbled as Margo helped her into a chair.

Abby stopped unbuttoning her coat for a moment as she met Margo's eye. "Oh, I think Pudgie is happier at home, Mimi."

"Home?" Mimi half laughed. "You call that dump a home?"

"That dump is costing—" Abby pinched her lips. "Never mind."

Oh, dear. Margo took her seat while Abby flagged down a busboy. "A bottle of Pinot Grigio," she said.

"I'll get your waiter," he replied.

"Oh, but you don't mind, do you? Just this once? It's been a day. And we're celebrating." Abby batted her lashes and, cheeks flushing, the poor young man muttered his agreement and hurried away.

"He's not the waiter, Abby," Margo scolded.

Abby just held her stare, her face impassive. "Tell me, could you have waited another fifteen minutes for something to take the edge off?"

Margo looked down at the scratch on her hand, which Pudgie had left there after first climbing and then jumping from the drapes to Margo's shoulder, much to

Mimi's endless delight.

"Pudgie was having so much fun!" Mimi said now. "He loves company."

Margo reached for her water. Abby was right. She did need a drink. "Yes, well, the party is over." While her grandmother sulked, Margo leaned across the table and hissed to her sister, "You really thought it would be a good idea to get her that cat?"

"Don't blame me!" Abby's eyes were wide. "She was lonely. I assumed a cat would be less work than a dog, not that they allow dogs at Serenity Hills. It isn't my fault that it has such a large personality."

A large personality. That was one way of phrasing it. Though she'd only met Pudgie twice, Margo could practically count the number of teeth in his mouth from his multiple attempts of nipping at her.

"He's not so bad, really," Abby continued. "I just think..."

At this moment, the waiter arrived with the wine, the young busboy close at his heels, his eyes fixed on Abby. Of course. Too young to serve. Not that this had stopped Abby from flirting with him to get her way.

"You were saying?" Margo pressed, after the waiter poured them each a glass and Abby had graciously bestowed a smile on the blushing busboy.

"I just don't think Pudgie likes you," Abby said, tipping her head in sympathy.

Was this what it had come to? They were discussing

the personal preferences of their grandmother's obese feline? "He can join the crowd," Margo muttered, taking a long sip of wine. It went down smooth. She caught Abby's suspicious look over the rim of her glass. "Well," she said, clearing her throat. She set down the glass and picked up the menu, even though the offerings hadn't changed in twenty-five years. "Should we start with calamari?"

But Abby wasn't biting. "Everything okay, Margo?"

"Of course!" Margo said, but it was no use. Her cheeks flushed and her glass rattled when she reached for the wine again. Her eyes began to dart all over the room, right to the door, where a crowd was gathered, waiting for a table to open up, and there, at the back of the group, was Eddie.

This night just got better and better.

"At least everything was okay up until a minute ago," she said. "Eddie's here."

Abby seemed to perk up at this, but then, she always loved a bit of drama. "Oh, and it looks like he's alone!"

Sure enough, Eddie was pushing his way through the crowd toward the bar. Margo picked up the menu again, hoping to hide behind it, but Mimi had other plans.

"Eddie! Eddie Boyd!" Mimi called, waving her hand high above her head.

"Mimi—" Margo said through gritted teeth, but it was too late. Eddie swiveled his head, finally finding the source of the voice. He glanced at Margo sharply, and spotting her, gave a hundred-watt grin.

Oh, for Pete's sake.

"Can't seem to stop running into you," he said as he approached the table.

"One of the perks of small-town life," she said, hoping he caught the sarcasm.

"Eddie Boyd! I have a bone to pick with you, young man!" Mimi reprimanded. Eddie's smile turned positively wicked now and Margo rolled her eyes to the ceiling, waiting for it.

"And what's that, Mrs. Harper?" Eddie said, leaning down to kiss one of her cheeks in greeting.

Mimi swatted him away, but a pleased smile pursed her red lipstick-painted mouth. "This here granddaughter of mine is now thirty-two years old, and she's not getting any younger! Have you seen those fine lines around her eyes?"

Eddie's own eyes danced. "Can't say that I have, but I can look again."

Margo scowled at him, but he studiously ignored her. Abby, of course, was beaming.

"Thirty-two years old and spending Saturday night with her sisters and grandmother. Tell me, how much longer until you make an honest woman out of her?"

Margo choked on her wine as Abby whooped in glee and Eddie did a poor job of covering his shock.

"Well, Mrs. Harper, your granddaughter is certainly a beautiful woman who stole my heart a long time ago, but I'm afraid she's already taken."

Margo set her glass back down. A beautiful woman. She knew she shouldn't feed into such trivial nonsense, but she couldn't help it. She hadn't been called that since…well, her wedding day, perhaps, and then it had been by her father. Ash wasn't one for compliments, and she supposed that when you were married, there was no need in stating the obvious attractions which helped bring you to that place to begin with. But hearing these words, spoken by Eddie. Well.

"That's right, Mimi," she said, struggling to say the words. "I'm married." Technically, and better for everyone at this table to go on thinking so. Especially Eddie, she thought, accidentally catching his eye.

Mimi was blinking hard, as if trying to remember something. "Oh, that's right. You left town. Broke my girl's heart."

Eddie's smile disappeared. "Well, now, it wasn't that simple."

"Wasn't it?" Margo knew she should let it rest, but she couldn't let him off the hook that easily.

He gave her a long, heated look, and this time she didn't break his stare. *Eddie. Oh, Eddie. Why'd you do it?* And did it matter? What was done was done. It could never be undone.

Her heart began to hurt, and she looked away, suddenly wishing she'd never come here at all. To The Lantern. To Oyster Bay.

"And then she went off and married that woman," Mimi finished.

Now Abby was giggling and Eddie's eyes were filled with mirth, but Margo was far from amused. "Mimi," she said with overt patience, or perhaps, lack thereof. "I told you. Ashley is a man."

"If you say so." Mimi snorted, giving her cohorts a wide-eyed stare.

Margo shook her head and lifted her wine glass. No use continuing this conversation. Besides, her mind wasn't on Ash right now. It was on what Eddie had said. About why he'd left. About how it wasn't so simple.

"Well, I should let you enjoy your evening," Eddie said. "I'm meeting a friend and I think Chip is on his way over here to give you the royal treatment."

Mimi sat up straighter at this, but Margo found herself wondering just who this friend Eddie had referred to could be. It was Saturday night, and Eddie wasn't married. His cousin Nick was apparently living in Portland, and he didn't have any other old friends in town. Was he waiting for a date?

She raked her eyes over his chest, wishing her stomach didn't tighten at the sight of those broad shoulders, and assessed his outfit. Jeans and a navy sweater under his coat. Anything was possible.

"Will I have the pleasure of seeing you ladies at the festival tomorrow?" he said as he turned to go.

"The Fall Fest," Abby explained, as if Margo didn't know, or had forgotten, which she refused to admit she had. The annual event had been one of her favorites growing up, after all.

"Wouldn't miss it," she said.

He grinned. "Good."

She didn't read into that either. She couldn't, because just then, a slightly older woman walked into the restaurant and called out Eddie's name, and then...Then the night was officially ruined.

*

Bridget stood in the front hallway of the McDowells' cedar-sided Colonial, feeling even worse than she had the last time Jeffrey and Trish had invited her over, that time under the guise of matching her up with their next-door neighbor—a perfectly pleasant man who wasn't shy in revealing that he hadn't gone on a date in the three years since he'd moved to town to be close to family, mostly in part because his mother needed him for dinner five nights a week. He then spent a half hour showing her pictures of his cat, Nutjob, something her sister Abby was still giggling about to this day.

Jeffrey and Trish were on a mission to set her up. She was their charity case. She got it. They were her oldest friends. They wanted her to be happy. Like them. They saw a problem and they wanted to fix it. And she was apparently a problem that needed fixing.

"Dinner was delicious as always," she said, wishing for not the first time that she could reciprocate the hospitality and invite her friends over for a meal for once. Trish had been there, of course, popping in to her apartment, and once she'd been sweet enough to watch Emma when Bridget had a late closing and Ryan wasn't able to get away from the bar to watch his kid for an hour. But there was something sad about inviting a couple, a couple with a big house and secure jobs and two sons, into her single-mother world. Abby said it was her issue, and maybe it was. But what Abby didn't understand was that it wasn't the square footage or the quality of the finishes that made Bridget hesitant to have people over. It was the fact that nothing about her apartment felt like home. It said nothing of her personality or her hopes or dreams. It spoke only of her circumstances. Her situation. And the future that she was supposed to have and didn't.

"Are you sure you don't want to take some leftovers home? That way you won't have to cook tomorrow night for Emma."

"I promised Emma I'd take her to the festival tomorrow. You guys going?"

"Of course!" Jeffrey said, throwing a casual arm around Trish's shoulder.

Bridget stifled a sigh. That shoulder could have just as easily been hers as much as this house might have been her home if she'd played her cards right and accepted that invitation to the school dance all those years ago. It wasn't that she was particularly attracted to Jeffrey, but then, attraction was clearly overrated, considering how things had turned out with Ryan.

She stepped toward the door. She was getting silly.

These were her friends. Her very happy and happily married friends, who were clearly meant to be, and it was best for them all that she had stepped back when she did. Trish was besotted with Jeffrey, and Jeffrey was such a good man, he deserved that. Their life had turned out the way it should have. And her life...Well, she didn't know the ending yet. And she told herself that this was okay. Even though some days, it didn't feel okay at all.

"I should get Emma," she said. It was ten minutes to eight, meaning she couldn't linger any longer even if she wanted to, and she did. Being with Trish and Jeff was always a good time, and their home was a perfect escape, not just because of the delicious food and overstuffed sofas near the crackling fireplace, but because it wasn't burdened with the endless responsibilities she felt when she walked through her own door.

Well now, she was feeling sorry for herself again, something she tended to do on the nights that Ryan had Emma.

She walked to the car, all too aware that Jeffrey and Trish were standing in the doorway, his arm still around her as they watched their poor single friend head out into the night on her own, as if she were their teenage daughter, not the girl who had shared a banana seat with Trish as they pedaled into town for bags of taffy after school.

She pulled her phone from her pocket to see if Ian Fowler had left any word yet, and frowned when she saw a message from Ryan instead. Mike, his bartender, had called in sick. He was at the pub. With Emma.

Bridget cursed under her breath as she pulled out of the driveway and gripped the steering wheel, cruising at a speed of five miles over the limit and mercifully hitting every green light on the way into town. Maybe she was overreacting. After all, this was Oyster Bay, and Ryan ran a gastro pub, not a strip joint, but she couldn't help it. Her eight-year-old little girl should have spent the night at the bowling alley, not sitting on a bar stool.

By the time she pushed by a group of rowdy guys hovering outside the front door and into the overly heated room, her heart was hammering in her chest. She didn't know who she hoped to see first—her daughter, so she could be sure she was all right, or her ex, so she could give him a piece of her mind.

Her eyes locked on Emma, sitting at the bar, of course, perched on a stool. A basket of fries was in front of her, and no doubt that was Ryan's latest lady friend at her side. Ryan didn't like the word girlfriend. It implied a commitment that was never there.

Bridget sized up the size-two blonde as she marched over to her daughter. Big boobs, fake tan, too much eye makeup. Yep. Ryan was painfully predictable. He'd only broken the mold once, and look how that turned out.

"Mommy!" Emma's face lit up just as the blonde's face fell. "Look! Daddy made me a kiddy cocktail."

Nice. When she was a kid they called them Shirley Temples.

"Where is your father?" she asked, her gaze drifting to the mound of fries that was, no doubt, Emma's dinner.

"He's *busy*," the blonde cut in, jutting her chin.

Too busy for his daughter? Bridget didn't blink. "And who are you? The babysitter?"

The girl narrowed her eyes. "I'll go find him."

Bridget knew she should say thank you, and the old Bridget would have—but that was before Emma, before another person became more important to her than herself. Back when her mistakes were hers alone.

Ryan came over to the bar, alone, Bridget noted. "What's wrong?" he asked, giving her one of those boyish grins that used to work on her and no doubt still did with the under twenty-five crowd.

She wasn't smiling. "Tonight is your night with Emma."

"Yes." Ryan nodded, trying his best to look earnest, but failing miserably. God, how she hated the way Ryan always managed to make her feel like a school marm, when she was just trying to be a responsible adult. One of them had to be.

"You're supposed to be spending time with her."

"I am spending time with her." He looked at her like she was half-crazy, and maybe she was. Crazy to have ever fallen for a guy like Ryan, who was all looks and charm and dreams. Crazy to ever think there would come a day when he didn't find a way to let her down.

"No, your flavor of the week is spending time with her."

Ryan's lips thinned. "Oh, so this is what it's really about."

"Excuse me?"

Ryan folded his arms across his chest shaking his head in disappointment. "I'm not going to apologize for moving on with my life. And I'll remind you that you left me."

Bridget felt a surge of anger that only Ryan could bring out in her. "You're right, Ryan. I did leave you. I left because then, like now, this pub was more important to you than me or Emma." She glanced over her shoulder, making sure that Emma was out of earshot, though it was a wonder anyone could hear anything from the noise in this place. "Do you have any idea how much Emma looks forward to these nights with you? She spent half the morning telling me how the two of you were going to go bowling and then out for ice cream."

The shame that darkened Ryan's eyes was brief. "I'm not going to apologize for having a job to do. I said in my message—"

Bridget held up a hand. "I know, I know. Mike was sick. And last time you got a last-minute party of twenty booked. And the time before that your kitchen was understaffed." She shook her head. "What'll it be next time?"

"She's having a good time," Ryan said.

"It's eight fifteen on a Saturday night and the two girls in the corner are slurring their words and doing shots."

Bridget was clenching her teeth so hard that her jaw ached. "And she's eight. She shouldn't be sitting in a bar."

"It's a restaurant that also has a bar," Ryan replied.

Bridget's mouth moved, but no sound came out, and maybe that was for the best. There was no point in trying to reason with Ryan. Hadn't she learned that years ago?

"I'm taking Emma home now," she replied.

"I'm supposed to have her until eight thirty," Ryan replied, but Bridget shot him a look and he said nothing more.

She moved toward the bar, but Ryan's hand was suddenly on her arm. She turned, bracing herself for an argument, but instead he gave her an apologetic smile. Another thing he'd mastered. "Why don't you stay and have something to eat?"

"I already ate," she said, refusing to feed into those puppy dog eyes, the very ones he used to give her when he said they'd have to wait to talk about a house next year, and next year became the year after that.

"Wait. There's something I wanted to talk to you about." His smile slipped, and he thrust his hands into the pockets of his jeans. He looked as contrite as the man could, which wasn't saying much.

Of course. He needed something. A loan. A favor.

"You've said enough for one night," she said, and walked over to Emma, whose cheek was now cupped in her palm, her eyelids drooping as her dirty blond hair dipped into the pool of ketchup next to her fries.

"Come on, honey," she said with forced cheer. "Time

to go home."

Emma's eyes immediately filled with tears. "But…but we didn't go bowling yet! Daddy promised!"

Your father promised me a lot of things, too, she wanted to say. Instead she said, "I'll take you bowling next weekend. Just us girls." It wasn't the same, and she didn't expect it to help, but it was the best she could offer. She took her daughter's hand and walked her to the door, and as she bundled her into the car, she knew there was only one thing worse than being disappointed by her ex: watching him disappointment their daughter, and knowing that there was nothing she could do to stop it.

Chapter Nine

The Fall Fest was an annual tradition in Oyster Bay, held the first weekend of October, rain or shine. When the girls were young, their parents would dress them in matching wool coats, something their mother was keen to do at holidays until Bridget grew too old for smocked dresses and began to protest dressing like Abby, who was six years her junior, after all. Back then, though, they didn't mind the coats, or the matching hats. They came to the festival with pumpkins they'd each picked out that morning and would decorate in the children's pumpkin contest. It was without saying that Margo, artistic from a young age, frequently won, much to Bridget's annoyance and Abby's dismay.

"I'm happy to see that you're entering the pumpkin contest, Emma," Margo said as she crossed the street to the town green with her sisters and niece. It was a chilly day, the salty breeze was blowing her ponytail, and she was especially grateful for the coat Bridget had lent her. She knew she should break down and buy herself one, but she couldn't justify the purchase, not when she had a perfectly nice wool coat at home. Buying one here would be admitting to herself that she didn't plan on returning, and that was too much to think about right now. It was easier to not think about Charleston or her house or her husband at all. Easier to fall into the routine of life here in Oyster Bay. It was Fall Fest. A day for hot cider and hay rides and binging on pumpkin spice doughnuts.

"I'm entering a contest today too," Abby announced with a grin.

"Oh, really?" Margo looked down to the brown paper bag her sister had been carrying all the way from Bridget's apartment. "What's in there?"

Abby seemed to hesitate, then stopped at a bench on the sidewalk. She reached into the bag and pulled out a beautiful apple pie, topped with a lattice crust that was sprinkled in sugar.

"You're entering the pie baking contest?" Bridget looked as surprised as Margo felt.

Abby nodded. "I saw the flier and well, it seemed like fun."

"Where'd you learn to do that?" Margo wondered if there was more that she'd missed in her absence than Mimi being sent to Serenity Hills.

Abby shrugged. "I like watching cooking shows and experimenting. Mimi taught me some of her recipes, too. I used to visit her and we'd cook together. Before she moved."

Bridget frowned. "I didn't know that." She looked almost hurt.

Abby carefully set the pie back in the bag. "Anyway, this was one of the last recipes we worked on together, so I thought…why not?"

Why not. It was such an Abby thing to say. Abby who had switched majors in college four times in as many years, barely pulling together enough credits to finish with a degree in Philosophy, which she'd never put to any real use. Abby who flitted from boyfriend to boyfriend, never really investing or caring if things didn't work out. Abby who was perfectly fine hopping from one job to the next, never committing to an actual career.

Margo suddenly envied her cavalier attitude, her ability to enjoy the moment and not worry about tomorrow. "Well, you have a good chance at winning if it tastes as good as it looks."

Abby just shrugged again. "We'll see!"

They had barely crossed the threshold of the green when Abby let out a whoop of delight and, rattling off an apology that was far from sincere, went hurrying across the lawn to where a band was setting up in the gazebo for the afternoon concert.

Margo watched with interest as Abby set down the bag, climbed the steps of the gazebo, and leaned in to embrace a man in a white T-shirt and faded jeans.

"He doesn't look as grungy as I'd imagined him," she observed.

Bridget rolled her eyes. "And by Thanksgiving, he'll be history. You know how Abby is."

Margo nodded. Sadly, she did. Ever since she was twelve, Abby had been boy crazy. She'd use her birthday money to subscribe to teen celebrity magazines and cover the walls in pinups of her current crush.

"She's as fickle about her career as she is about the men she dates," Bridget sighed. "You know that job at the doctor's office won't last until Thanksgiving either."

Margo wished she could believe otherwise, but Bridget had a point. Abby would soon claim she was bored, or behave in a way that indicated just how bored she was, which would lead to termination—something that had happened at the dentist's office, the insurance agency, and a handful of other places off the top of her head.

"Abby needed parents," Margo said, feeling bad. "We were lucky we had them for as long as we did."

"I tried to guide her," Bridget said, taking the pumpkin out of Emma's sagging arms. "But she was in college by then and didn't want to listen to my advice. I think she resented me for not being Mom."

Margo nodded. "She'll never admit how much she misses them."

"I miss them every day," Bridget said, blinking quickly as she looked away.

Margo didn't reply. The ache in her chest wouldn't let her. It was just the problem with Oyster Bay—she may be able to escape her marital troubles here, but all the other painful parts of her life were front and center and unavoidable.

"How was the showing?" she asked instead, even though a part of her didn't want to know.

"Oh, fine." Bridget shrugged. "Not much to tell. He'll get back to me."

"Did he seem interested?"

Bridget gave a little smile. "For a moment, I thought he was interested in me." She laughed, but not happily. "He's engaged."

Ah. As far as Margo knew, Bridget had never dated since her divorce from Ryan. She never complained about it, or made it seem like she even wanted a romantic life. Now Margo wondered if her sister was lonely, and the thought of it made her sad. If she had lived closer, she could have stopped by for dinner more often, taken Bridget out to get her nails done, let her have a little time to pamper herself.

Guilt weighed heavy as they walked toward the site of the pumpkin decorating contest, where dozens of children were already seated and hard at work. Bridget set Emma's pumpkin on a picnic table and guarded it while Emma ran to the supply table to select her decorations. She returned with markers, glitter, glue, pom poms, and multiple sheets of stickers. "I think I'm going to win for sure," she said, beaming as she slid onto the bench.

"She's precious," Margo said to Bridget, for the first time wondering if Ash's betrayal would have been easier if she had a daughter to look after, or if that would have just made things worse.

"You and Ash thinking of having kids anytime soon?"

Margo swallowed the lump in her throat. "I don't think so," she said, realizing the horrible truth in her statement. She looked away, across the crowded green, to where Abby was still chatting with her man friend. "Abby really seems to like this guy. Don't you think she'll ever settle down?"

"Oh, I don't know." Bridget led them to a bench under a maple tree that was just starting to turn, its leaves becoming a vibrant orange. She kept one eye on Emma, who was so engrossed in her project, she hadn't even noticed her mother step away. "I'm not sure Abby has what it takes, honestly. Marriage is hard."

"You're telling me," Margo replied before she could stop herself.

Bridget looked at her sidelong. "How is Ash? You haven't mentioned him much."

"Not much to tell," Margo said, but damn it, her voice was shrill. There was a lot to tell, but that would require thinking about it, stirring up the hurt and the sadness, the humiliation and the anger.

Her professor husband was shagging his law student. Her life had become a cliché.

"Do you really miss not being married?" she dared to ask, thinking of what Bridget had said the other night at her apartment. She and Bridget rarely discussed the divorce, only loosely, in terms of her continued tense relationship with Ryan.

Bridget shook her head. "Not to Ryan. He was never the marrying kind, and I refused to see that. Sometimes it's easier to see what you want to see, I suppose."

Margo understand all too well. It was easier to think of her relationship with Ash as safe and easy and comfortable, not looking too closely at the truth of the situation. Was it really normal to eat dinners in silence each night, or in front of the evening news, before going off for the evening to separate quarters of the house? Where was the laughter, the spontaneity, the joy? Even when they went out, they kept things polite, peaceful. Low conflict. They never argued. She hadn't even said anything when he gave his mother a gold locket for Christmas last year and bought Margo a new gardening spade; instead she'd told herself he knew how hard she'd been trying with those rose bushes...

She sighed. There had been red flags, lots of them now that she was willing to look for them.

"Don't look now, but I think Eddie Boyd is trying to get your attention." Bridget wiggled her eyebrows as Margo felt herself pale in panic.

He'd said he was coming, and okay, fine, she did wear her best sweater in case he actually did show up, but did she really want to talk to him again?

Yes, she decided, looking subtly over her shoulder to where he stood. She did want to talk to Eddie. She was confronting the truth in her relationships at long last, and she'd like some answers from him once and for all.

*

"Hey," he said, giving her a slow smile as she walked over to him.

Margo took a measured breath, counted to three. "Hey." There. That wasn't so bad.

"I wasn't sure if you'd be here." His eyes were clear in the afternoon sunlight, his green sweater bringing out the flecks of color around his pupils. She tried to look away and found it difficult. When Eddie stared at her like that, she'd always found it hard to stay angry at him for long.

"Are you kidding? Fall Fest was one of the highlights of my childhood, I'll have you know."

"And here I thought it was the Christmas Carnival," he bantered.

"Oh." He had a point, and the realization that he remembered this, and that Ash probably couldn't tell the difference between the two events, even after ten years of marriage, made her uneasy.

"Well, I don't like to pick favorites," she replied. "I love everything about Oyster Bay."

He lifted an eyebrow. "Seriously?"

He really did know her too well. "No."

There was more she could say—ask him what he was doing back, why he was here, why he had returned now and not then, when he said he would. Instead she looked around the festival, wondering if their conversation was about to be cut short. "You here alone?"

He nodded. "But I think my aunt and uncle are here somewhere."

"I'm here with my sisters," she informed him, realizing by the lack of surprise in his eyes how lame that sounded. "I wasn't sure if you'd be here with the woman from last night."

His brow creased for a long moment until his eyes burst open in surprise. "Sylvia?"

Was that her name? Margo felt a sense of dread. Of course he was attached. Did she honestly think she was the only one of them who had moved on?

"Sylvia's my partner," he said, starting to laugh. "She has three unruly sons and a husband who left her for a skinnier version. I took her out last night because it was her birthday, and she was breaking her diet for your uncle's chowder."

"Oh," Margo said, feeling far more pleased than she should. She should empathize with Sylvia, feel sorry for her even. "That was really nice of you to do that."

Very adult of him, she thought, frowning a little.

"Come on," he said, jutting his chin to the food stands which were lined up on the west side of the green. "Can I buy you a drink?"

Suddenly it all became too clear that Eddie was, in fact, single. And this fact was almost more dangerous than him being back in town. Almost more dangerous that the fact every time he looked at her, her heart sped up. She hesitated, wondering what she was agreeing to, even dared to think of Ash for a fleeting moment. But then she remembered Candy. And then she remembered Abby, and her motto. "Why not?" she said, with a smile.

They stopped at Hollow Tree Farm's food truck and ordered two ciders, one hard, one fresh pressed.

Before Margo could say anything, Eddie said, "I don't drink."

Margo sipped her cider. Back when she knew Eddie, they were both too young to drink. Had something happened in the time since he'd left? It saddened her. All this time she'd oscillated between worry and anger. Was Eddie okay? And if he was, why hadn't he ever contacted her again?

"You don't need to explain," she said.

"It's okay," he said easily. "Do you know why I was at Serenity Hills the other day?"

Margo's cheeks flared when she thought of the way she'd run from him. She opened her mouth to explain, but it was no use. His eyes glinted with mischief now.

"I saw you run away from me," he said, giving her a long look.

"Well, it was either that or shove my ninety-year-old grandmother into the broom closet," she said, but she was laughing now. "I'm sorry. I was just surprised to see you there."

"I was visiting my dad," he said, and Margo did a poor job of hiding the shock in her expression. "I know. It's…I don't know what it is," he finally said, burying his face in his plastic cup.

"I didn't know you were in touch with him," she said, and then realized how presumptuous that was. It had been more than a decade since she'd spoken to Eddie. A lot could change in that amount of time.

She glanced at him, taking in the man beside her, so different from that boy he'd once been, she realized. Yep, a lot could change.

"We got back in touch a long time ago," he said, and then faded into silence again. Margo waited for him to say more, but he had a distant look in his eyes. "Then we lost touch again. I didn't hear from him again until last year. That's why I moved back to Oyster Bay."

"I don't follow," Margo said. Last she knew, Eddie had been sent to Oyster Bay to live with his father's brother and his wife because his dad was "in trouble." Whatever the trouble was, Eddie had never let on and Margo hadn't pushed. She'd heard rumors, of course. Oyster Bay was full of gossip. Some people said Eddie's dad was in prison. Others said he was a gambler, that he'd run off to

Vegas and was dead broke. Margo hadn't cared what they said about Eddie's father, and she still didn't. She'd only cared about Eddie…and, she realized with a sinking feeling, she still did.

"My dad has sclerosis of the liver," Eddie said frankly. He stopped walking, looking her square in the eye. "His brother's the only family he's got other than me, and my uncle took him in, set him up in Serenity Hills. Tracked me down and asked me to come back."

"I'm sorry, Eddie." She wanted to reach out, set a hand on his arm, hold his hand. Hug him. But that wasn't her place anymore. Once, it had been, when the teasing at school got bad, and the hurt in his eyes was deep. She'd smile and lead him away, and they'd make their own good time, and leave all that other stuff behind them. When he wanted to open up, she listened, but she never pried. There were parts of his story she knew: how his mother had left him earlier than he could even remember her, that his father had a temper, and they always ran out of money, and that he'd been shipped to Oyster Bay against his will, but that really, his uncle and aunt and even Nick were pretty great. Deep down, Margo had always sensed that Eddie was a lot happier to be in Oyster Bay than he'd ever admit. Maybe even to himself.

"It's difficult to accept that this is how it ends," he said. "All this time, I guess a part of me hated him, but another part of me longed for something that wasn't there, and…hoped that someday it could be found."

Margo dropped onto a bench, and Eddie sat beside her. "But you were in touch with him before, you said."

"After I left Oyster Bay," Eddie said. "That's when things took a turn for the worse."

Margo looked at him sharply. "Worse? How?"

"I know the detention center was supposed to straighten me out, but…" Eddie shrugged. "I lasted two weeks before they called my uncle. He said he would spare my aunt by not telling her, said it would break her heart. Instead, my uncle called my dad. Ray came, picked me up, and that was that." He gave her a wry look.

"What happened?" Margo asked.

"Oh, it was fine at first," Eddie said. "We went home, I got a job bagging groceries to help pay the rent. But then the drinking started and the poker games, and one night he was feeling lucky, went all in."

Margo didn't like where this story was headed. "Let me guess."

"Lost it all. Every dime he'd saved and I'd worked for. Man, he went on a bender that time. I didn't see him for three days, and when I did…let's just say he wasn't happy to see me. Said I was bad luck, that I wasn't earning my keep. I left that night."

"Why didn't you come back to Oyster Bay?" Why, why? She would have taken him in; they could have found a way.

"My uncle wouldn't have me. My chances were up."

And me? she wanted to ask. It was right there, on the tip of her tongue. But the sadness in his eyes stopped her.

"Life was hard for a while. I fell in with a bad crowd, started drinking... I guess you could say that I gave up on myself for a while."

"I hadn't given up on you," Margo said quietly.

He held her gaze. "I wasn't coming back to Oyster Bay, Margo. I wasn't going anywhere."

She understood, even if she wished it could have been different. "You could have called me. Maybe it would have helped."

He shook his head. "Wouldn't have changed a damn thing."

"No," she said eventually, "I suppose not."

"I couldn't bring you into that mess," Eddie said. "I wanted to...but I couldn't. Does that make sense?"

She could only nod. In a way it did. Of course it did.

"It all worked out in time. I stopped drinking, got my GED, eventually joined the force. Not to say I didn't struggle for a while," he added. He'd finished his cup and he stood to toss it in the trash can. "Well, now you know."

Yes, she thought, feeling no better than she had yesterday, and maybe worse. Now she knew.

*

Eddie didn't know why he was telling her all of this. To defend himself? Apologize? Maybe a little of both.

"I guess it's funny in a way," he mused. "You never know how life will end up."

And he still didn't, he thought, thinking of Mick's invitation. It had been weighing on him ever since Friday, settling heavily on his shoulders, and only disappearing for fleeting moments before returning with full force. There was no one he could tell: his uncle and aunt would encourage him to stay, to be with his father. And Sylvia would probably hit the vending machines hard and then blame him for it later. He was her partner. How could he forsake her?

But then Mick was his partner, too. His friend. The first real friend he'd ever had, really.

Other than Margo.

"No, you never can tell how things will end," Margo said, her voice a little sad. "You can only react to the moment, I suppose. And have faith."

Something in the way she said that last sentence made him question if she had any left. "Well, everything turned out okay in the end," he said, but from the emptiness in Margo's eyes he wasn't so sure about that.

"I wish I could say that was true," Margo replied, looking down at her drink. "I caught my husband with another woman. Well, a girl really. Barely legal," she mumbled, taking a long sip of her drink. "Her name is Candy. She wears pearls. And her hair bounces."

He struggled not to show his surprise.

"What a bastard," he finally said. Margo was sweet and smart and still so beautiful. What man would take that granted?

He knew he never did.

"Well, now you know why I'm back in Oyster Bay," she said, sighing. "Guess you could say I'm sort of at a crossroads."

"Are you thinking of staying?" There was hope in his voice that didn't have any business being there, but he couldn't help it. He wanted her to stay. Oyster Bay didn't feel right without her. She'd been his friend, his best friend, and so much more than that. She'd been the bright spot in a dark time. He'd always love her for that.

"I don't know," she said, searching his face. "Coming here...nothing's the same."

"Well, you're not the same," he pointed out.

She considered this for a moment. "True. I'm bitter now. Hard." She winked at him, her mouth twisting into a little smile, and he laughed.

"You've grown up. Had experiences that shaped you. You'll get through this," he said.

"I hope you're right," she said. She didn't look convinced.

"Honey, I'm always right," he joked, hoping to lighten the mood.

She blinked, but her smile shone in her eyes. "Oh yeah? Name one time."

He hesitated, thinking back on the most recent time. "What I told you that last day, before I left for New Jersey. Do you remember what I said?"

Her smile slipped. She pulled on her ponytail, twirling it in her hands, avoiding eye contact. "Oh. I..."

But he wasn't going to let this go. Not now, not when they were sitting side by side. When he didn't know if they would ever sit like this again.

"I told you that we'd be together again." He'd said other things, too. That he loved her. That he always would. "Seems to me by the way we're sitting here talking that I was right about that."

"Eddie." Margo's voice caught, and her eyes had welled with tears.

"It's okay," he said. "We don't need to talk about that time anymore. We're here now. Older and wiser."

"Yes," she said, lowering her eyes. "We're here now."

Who would have ever thought that? It wasn't until years after he'd left Oyster Bay that he reached out to his aunt and uncle again, as part of his steps, finding forgiveness. By then Margo was married; his aunt had told him, regret in her voice. His heart had sunk then, even though he figured a girl like Margo would be swooped up and that he was lucky to have ever had her as his at all. And yet here he was. And here she was. So close that he could reach out, touch her cheek, brush away the tear that had started to fall. He inched forward, wanting to hold her, kiss her, maybe just wrap an arm around her. "Margo…"

She pulled back, stood quickly, alarm in her eyes. "I should go find Bridget and Abby. I promised I'd be there for the pie judging contest."

"Margo," Eddie started, but she was backing up.

"I should go," she said, and he said nothing more, but watched from the bench as she became smaller and smaller in the distance, the way she had that terrible, awful day all those years ago.

Chapter Ten

The light on Bridget's work phone was flashing when she walked into her office, thermos of coffee in hand, at quarter past nine on Monday morning.

Maybe it was the string of bad luck she seemed to have lately, but her very first thought was that this couldn't be good.

Her mind flitted through a mental rolodex of possibilities as she dropped her bag on one of the two visitor chairs that faced her desk and hung her coat on the hook behind her door. The lone plant she kept in the corner was sagging, probably from lack of light, considering she was stuck in a back, windowless room. The better offices were reserved for the three other agents in the firm, the ones who were able to move product on a regular basis.

She sank into her chair, feeling that familiar weight of frustration and failure that she just couldn't seem to shake, and stared at the blinking light. It could be Serenity Hills, calling to say that Mimi had let Pudgie roam the hallways. Again. Or it could be something worse this time...

It could be the school nurse, calling to say that Emma was running a fever, but considering that Bridget had just come from dropping her off at Oyster Bay Elementary, this didn't seem very likely.

It could be Abby, calling to say she'd lost yet another job. Or Ryan, wanting to talk. And Ryan wanting to talk was never a good thing.

It could be a bill collector. She was never behind on rent or bills, but she'd never gotten over the time when she was still married and Ryan failed to send in the payment for the electric bill, using the money instead to fund some new appliances at the pub, and one day, the lights had all gone out in the middle of winter. The heat, too. That was years ago, but it still haunted her.

Years ago, she told herself firmly. She was no longer financially bound to Ryan. Their past could no longer hurt her.

With that, she picked up the receiver and pressed a button to retrieve her messages. Maybe she'd be pleasantly surprised, and if not, well, she was certainly prepared.

But it wasn't Mimi, or Emma's school, or Ryan or

Abby who needed her attention right now. The message was from Ian Fowler. He was ready to make an offer.

Bridget dropped the phone onto the receiver as if it were burning her hand. She pushed back her chair, creating distance between herself and the phone and everything that Ian had said in his message. Her heart was pounding as she stared at her half-dead plant in the corner.

She stood up. Coffee. She needed coffee. Then she remembered the thermos on her desk.

Fresh coffee then. Better yet: fresh air.

She'd treat herself, walk down to Angie's Café. After all, she could afford it now that Ian Fowler was buying the house and she was getting a nice commission. Normally she pursed her lips at the people she saw clutching paper cups from the café, thinking how far that extra five bucks a day could go over time—enough to pay for a half-hour piano lesson each week for Emma.

Now she could afford those lessons. And she was meeting the young couple in search of "clean lines" later this afternoon. With two sales under her belt this quarter and the savings she'd stashed away since the divorce, she might just be on her path toward getting a house of her own, soon.

The thought should over joy her, make her do a little happy dance right here in her office, but instead she felt deflated, heavy hearted, and on the brink of tears. Even the thought of telling Emma she could have the piano lessons did little to settle the queasy feeling in her stomach. After all, what good were lessons without a piano to play them on? The house would be sold, and the piano would too.

Her father's piano, she thought, her vision blurring. The one he used to play as a child, and later, as a father, especially on rainy summer nights when the girls were all stuck in the house and bored. He had a song for each of them. They didn't have names—he made them up.

She closed her eyes now, trying to bring the tune he played for her to the surface. Reaching for it. Aching for it.

Right. She needed a distraction. For the first time, she didn't want to think or over think. She wanted to…avoid.

She called Abby. From the grogginess of her sister's voice, it was clear that the call had woken her. At nine thirty.

Bridget struggled not to roll her eyes. Abby was content to live day by day, somehow scraping up rent for her studio apartment each month with part-time work, riding a bike instead of driving a car, and asking Bridget to trim her hair every other month in exchange for free babysitting. When Bridget had been Abby's age, she'd been a single working mother with a toddler.

"Did I wake you?"

"No, no, I'm awake, just stretching." Abby let out a luxurious groan.

Stretching. More like code for just waking up.

"What time is it?" Abby asked.

Now Bridget was really regretting this call. She'd been up since five to do laundry and shower. She'd started the slow cooker for dinner. She'd ironed Emma's favorite dress for picture day. She'd cooked a pancake breakfast. She'd cleaned the kitchen after Emma spilled batter all over the counter, braided Emma's hair, remembered to pack the library books so Emma could check out two new ones, filled out a field trip permission slip, answered three calls from Mimi, packed Emma's lunch while listening to her grandmother alternate between bragging about that damn cat and asking when Bridget was going to take her home.

And now Bridget would have to be the one to tell her that there was no home. That she'd sold it. And then she'd have to hope to God that Mimi remembered that she had agreed to this in the not so distant past.

"Want to meet for coffee?"

"Sure!" Abby sounded so pleased by the idea that for a moment, Bridget felt guilty. Was it really such a rare occurrence for her to invite her youngest sister to something, just the two of them?

Sadly, it was. But then, when did Bridget have the time for things like coffee dates? When she wasn't taking care of Emma, she was at work trying to make money to care for Emma, and even then she was cramming in weekly responsibilities like grocery shopping and visits to Mimi, who thought she was Margo half the time, even though they looked nothing alike.

"Margo, you always take such good care of me," Mimi

was fond of saying, and Bridget would fight back tears that she knew were childish and irrational, wishing that just for once she could get a thank you for everything she did for everyone else, or at least some credit.

But that was her role. They all had one. She was the mother hen, especially now that her own mother was gone. She was the only mother in the group, after all, and the oldest sister, and she cared. She cared so much. Too much.

"I'm surprised you have time to meet up!" Abby said now. There wasn't a hint of malice in her tone, only honesty, but Bridget felt as if she'd just been slapped. Abby's life was one long string of fun. She didn't understand Bridget's life. But it saddened Bridget that she couldn't. That she took Bridget's lack of time for her personally.

Her walk to the café was long, even if it was only three blocks away. She took her time, stopping to look at the storefronts that were decorated with bright purple and orange mums and fat pumpkins and colorful wreaths on every door. The bells above the door of Angie's jingled as she entered the room, and her spirits rose slightly at the smell of cinnamon scones and percolating coffee. She grabbed the last available table near the window, settling in for the wait, but a few minutes later, Abby rolled by on her bike.

Her sister's hair was pulled back in a casual knot, her face free of makeup, her bright green pea coat unbuttoned over her sweater and jeans.

She hopped out of bed to have coffee with me, Bridget realized, startled. When was the last time she'd dropped everything for Abby?

Bridget left her coat on the back of her chair and joined Abby at the counter, where she treated them both to an oversized blueberry muffin and latte, wishing she still had her sister's metabolism.

"God, I'm hungry," Abby said, grinning as she slid into her chair and shook off her coat. "I was out with Chase last night and he offered to cook, and…"

Oh dear God. "And you didn't want to get food poisoning?" Bridget would never, ever forget the time Chase had treated Abby to a bag of croissants he had later revealed were plucked from this very café's dumpster.

"No." Abby pressed her lips together. "I didn't want to hurt his feelings. So I said that I'd already eaten." Catching Bridget's disapproving look, Abby said, "He doesn't believe in waste, Bridget. Do you know how much food is thrown out every day? Not all of it is trash."

Bridget wasn't up for this conversation again. Not this morning. "So you're still dating Chase, then. It's been a while, then. A couple of months?"

"Well…" And there was the look. The look that said Abby was bored and ready for something new. The same exact look she used to get when she was just six years old and ready to quit a board game she wasn't winning. "I think we're going to break up." At this, to Bridget's surprise, Abby's eyes welled with tears that began to fall faster than Bridget could hand her paper napkins from the dispenser.

"Was it because..." Bridget trailed off. There were so many ways to finish that thought, but those were qualities that had drawn Abby to him, not away from him.

"He's going on the road," Abby sniffed. "With the band."

Oh. Well, yes, that made sense, considering Chase lived in his van. What choice was there but to keep moving?

"He's going to Florida," Abby continued. "Says the climate is better for his lifestyle."

The mother in Bridget wanted to tell Abby that if Chase really loved her, he would stay. That she was better knowing all this now, better off without him in the long run. That a guy like this would only cause her grief. But the sister in her just handed over another napkin and said, "I'm so sorry, Abby. I know you really liked him."

Abby would probably use the word *love*, but considering she'd only known the guy for two months, Bridget couldn't get on board with that. The beginning was the fun part. It was based on attraction and excitement and going out and trying new things. Not the real stuff. Not the hard stuff.

"He asked me to go with him," Abby said, eyeing her across the table.

Bridget's heart began to pound. Sure, Abby was annoying sometimes, carefree to a fault, even a little reckless, some might say. She certainly wasn't any help when it came to worrying about things like the cost of Mimi's care, or how to handle the house. But to leave?

Too many people had left already.

Bridget took a sip of her coffee, burying her face in the mug so Abby couldn't see the emotion in her eyes.

"I said no, obviously," Abby said, plucking a blueberry from her muffin. "Oyster Bay is my home. I could never leave it."

Bridget smiled. "I'm happy to hear that."

"I'd miss you. And Emma. And Mimi, of course. But I'll miss Chase." Abby gave a little shrug. "Who knows if I'll ever meet anyone else." She gazed dramatically out the window.

Bridget pinched her mouth. She'd give it until Thanksgiving, maybe even Halloween before Abby was professing her love again.

"I guess since we're making announcements, I have one too." She drew a deep breath. Was this really happening? Was she really going to say that she was selling the house?

Abby gasped as her hands flew to her mouth. "Oh my God! You met someone. *Finally*."

Bridget gave her a long look. "No. I did not meet someone. I got an offer on the house."

Abby had the nerve to look disappointed. "That's all?"

"That's *all*? That's our childhood home, Abby." She had expected tears, maybe even an outburst. Certainly not disappointment of all things.

Abby's expression was quizzical. "But I thought you wanted to sell it?"

"*Needed* to sell it," Bridget corrected. "No one *wants* to sell it. But the taxes and upkeep are too expensive, and besides, Mimi's room at Serenity Hills is far from free."

"Have you told Margo yet?" Abby asked, and Bridget groaned.

"No, and I'm dreading it." She took a sip of her latte, buying time. She and Abby weren't as close as she and Margo were; their age difference seemed to play a bigger part than physical distance in many ways. They didn't often have heart to heart talks, and Abby struggled to understand the root of the matter, it often seemed, but she also told things like they were. She was frank, and right now Bridget appreciated that honesty. "Do you think there's something going on with Margo?"

Abby jutted her bottom lip as she considered this. "Like what?"

Bridget looked out the window as a gust of wind stirred up the fallen leaves. They swirled in the air before falling again, bright bursts of gold on the pavement. "I don't know. I get the impression that something is troubling her."

"Has she said anything?"

"No," Bridget admitted.

"Well, she's not happy about the house being sold. It came as quite a shock to her," Abby pointed out.

"True." Bridget considered that Margo's visit had

started on a rough note. Perhaps that was all it was. After all, what could really be wrong in Margo's life? She had a big house, a wonderful, fulfilling job, and a responsible and settled husband.

"I guess I'll have to break the news to her soon," Bridget sighed.

"You're making the right choice," Abby said. "And really, what choice is there?"

Bridget marveled at her sister, who for all her silliness could be surprisingly wise.

"I suppose we've all moved on," she said, even though a part of her wasn't so sure that was true. Her heart would always be in that home, even if that phase of her life was behind her now.

"So you didn't meet anyone?" Abby tried again, and Bridget didn't know whether to laugh or cry.

Given the circumstances, she decided to laugh.

*

Margo walked into town for a late lunch, telling herself it was because of her rumbling stomach, but she couldn't lie, especially to herself.

She'd spent half the morning unfolding and refolding her meager belongings, wrestling with whether or not to call Ash, to have the big conversation, the one she could have had last week if she'd stayed around long enough for him to come home as if nothing was amiss.

The walk was about half a mile, but today she didn't mind the wind. It was fall in Oyster Bay, and that meant bright, warm colors, and the crunch of leaves under her feet. By the time she got to the café, her fingers were stiff and red. She thrust them into her pockets as she studied her options at the counter—finally deciding on a turkey sandwich on one of Angie's buttery and flaky croissants, with an Earl Grey tea to warm her up.

With her order placed, she wound her way through the crowded tables to the back corner, nodding and smiling at the familiar faces of people she'd grown up with or casually known around town, people who were born and raised in Oyster Bay and would never leave. There was the librarian, who still wore her hair in a long grey braid, and Bonny Brenner, who used to babysit the girls on the rare occasions when Mimi wasn't able to. Bonny was a grandmother now herself, from the looks of the two chubby-cheeked toddlers squabbling over a fudge brownie. And there was Dottie Joyce.

And it was too late to turn and run.

Dottie Joyce was the town historian. A role she took a bit too literally when it came to keeping track of the lives of all the residents of Oyster Bay. She had a knack for getting information out of people, which she attributed to her keen research skills. Margo's mother called her harmless. Margo's father called her bluff. And Margo…well, Margo was thinking that now might be the time to call Ash, just to have some way of looking busy.

She settled into a chair, avoiding direct eye contact as she draped her borrowed coat over the back. She faced the window, wishing she'd had the sense to bring a magazine or a book from the pile she'd found in a trunk back at the cottage, when a tapping on her shoulder made her jump.

"Jesus!" she exclaimed, putting a hand to her racing heart.

"They swear like that down south?" Dottie's blue eyes were round and wide.

"Hello, Dottie," Margo said through a tight smile that she hoped passed for pleasant. She glanced around the room, wishing Bonny would make eye contact and save her. Unfortunately the younger of the two children took that opportunity to wail, and all attention went to soothing things him.

"I heard you were in town," Dottie continued. "Staying at the cottage down near the harbor?"

"That's right," Margo said, saying nothing more.

Dottie didn't back down easily. "Your husband didn't come with you this time?"

Margo stifled a sigh and mentally rehearsed her excuse about Ash. "Afraid he was stuck at work."

"He doesn't miss you? You've been here almost a week," Dottie pressed, and this time Margo struggled to keep her smile.

"A little time apart never hurt anyone," Margo replied in what she hoped was a breezy tone. She kept her smile fixed. "Besides, he'd get bored with all the girl talk with my sisters, no doubt."

"Yes, it's just the Harper women in Oyster Bay now,

isn't it?" Dottie's smile widened. "And do you plan on staying much longer?"

Dottie waited patiently for Margo to answer, and Margo saw no choice. "Probably a little longer," she said lightly.

Dottie inched her chair a little closer and lowered her voice. "Well, then, perhaps you might be of service to me. I've lived in my home for thirty-five years. It's a historical landmark, you know."

Margo knew. She nodded, wondering where Dottie was going with this.

"Well, it needs a bit of freshening up. Nothing major. But...I was wondering if you might give your professional opinion? I'll pay you, of course."

Well, this was a surprise, and a pleasant one at that. "I'd love to come by your house, Dottie," she said, feeling her spirits lift. "Would tomorrow afternoon work for you?"

"Two o'clock?" Dottie looked pleased.

"Two is perfect," Margo said as she stood to collect her order from the counter. Strangely she was happy it had taken as long as it did to prepare. A new project was just what she needed right now, and not just because she could use the money. Creative work always took away her troubles, even if Dottie was a fair bit of trouble herself.

Chapter Eleven

At two o'clock the next afternoon, Margo stood on the steps of Dottie's yellow-painted Colonial, questioning just how desperate she was to have agreed to this meeting. She should be thinking about her future, and how she was going to handle things with Ash, not standing outside the house of Oyster Bay's nosiest local. She was avoiding her problems, she didn't need a therapist to tell her that.

Or maybe, just maybe, in a way that didn't exactly feel familiar, she was trying to move on.

She didn't know which was worse, honestly.

She was just considering turning around and hightailing it back to the cottage where she could hide from everything and everyone and pretend that nothing was happening, that nothing had to be dealt with or avoided, when the door swung upon and there was

Dottie, her blue eyes as round as ever.

"Margo!" Dottie seemed a little breathless. "Come, come in."

Margo had to admit she was a bit curious. Dottie Joyce had lived alone in this big old house near the center of town for as long as she could remember. Her husband, Arnie, supposedly died in a fishing accident, but details on that were surprisingly vague.

She stood in the center hallway and removed her ballet flats, wishing she wasn't now barefoot in the woman's home.

If Dottie noticed, she didn't seem to care. She was far more interested in taking Margo by the elbow and leading her into the front living room.

Which was covered from floor to ceiling in birds.

"I call this, the aviary room," Dottie said, glancing nervously at Margo, as if searching for approval.

Margo knew she had to say something, but her jaw was slack and no sound was coming out and...Oh, my God, some of the birds were real. In the corner of the room sat an enormous cage, where three birds sat on a perch. But that wasn't all. There were birds on the throw pillows. Birds on the drapes. Birds on the wallpaper. There were framed prints of birds and even the area rug had a pattern of...birds.

"You've really followed a theme in here," she said politely. Her eyes darted over the room, trying to take it all in.

"But not just in here!" Dottie danced over to the pocket doors and flung them open to reveal a bright pink dining room. Full of birds.

"I love birds," she gushed.

Margo swallowed. "I can see that."

"I got my first bird when I was a teenager," Dottie said eagerly, opening a curio cabinet full of bird figurines and almost reverently lifting a porcelain dove. "I call him Sweetheart."

Margo's eyes widened a notch. "He has a name?"

"Oh, they all have names!" Dottie said gaily.

"This is quite the collection," Margo said, nodding.

"Over ten thousand in total," Dottie said, carefully setting her figurine back on the shelf. "Whenever I go anywhere, I can't help myself. I have to buy a bird."

"It's certainly a conversation starter," Margo said. She was quickly running out of diplomatic things to say.

"Yes, but not everyone understands my passion," Dottie said, her expression darkening. "Arnie didn't like the birds. Said he preferred fish." She snorted at that, and led Margo into the kitchen, which was bird-free with the exception of a few faux bird houses hanging from the ceiling.

"Lately, I've been thinking that I need a better way to display my birds," Dottie said, proffering Margo a plate of cookies, which appeared to be homemade.

She'd made an effort, Margo realized, feeling strangely touched. And she was looking for Margo's approval, or guidance, or perhaps both.

"I think I can help you, Dottie," she said, alarm bells going off in her mind as Dottie's face lit up.

"I don't want to give up any of my birds, though," Dottie said, looking worried.

"No, of course not, but you want the rooms to be functional, and it sounds like you're looking for a change."

"I am." Dottie bit into a cookie thoughtfully. "I love my birds. But...well, I've been surrounded by them for so long. And then I went over to Estelle Hancock's house last month for the historical society meeting and well, her house felt so much less...cluttered."

Margo latched on to this. "Was there anything else you liked about Estelle's house?"

The Hancocks had been in Oyster Bay for generations, and their house was a favorite on the Harper girls' annual Halloween run. Not only did Estelle give out full-sized candy bars, but they also always invited the girls in for hot cider to warm up a bit.

"I liked the color scheme. It felt very light and airy."

It was true that Dottie's rooms were dark, and very one note when it came to color. The living room was navy and hunter and the mauve pink had been used in the dining room from the seat cushions to the wallpaper to the curtains.

"What if we designate one room to the birds?" Margo watched Dottie carefully, gauging her reaction. "Then it could be a true..." What was that word Dottie had used?

Oh, yes. "Aviary."

Dottie was nodding slowly, still clutching her cookie. "I like that idea."

"And that way we can spruce up the other rooms without having to be authentic to the colors of the...birds."

She could just imagine how Abby would react when she heard this.

"Do you have a spare bedroom?"

"Already filled with birds," Dottie said with a shrug.

So there were even more. "We might designate just one of the bedrooms then..."

Dottie raised an eyebrow. "If they'll fit. Those rooms are packed full. The downstairs might be better. More accessible."

Margo nodded. "Noted."

"I'll leave the birds in my bedroom," Dottie said. "They keep me company."

Margo blinked. Was this her future? A spinster who collected birds?

"We'll do the living room and dining room," Margo said. "Unless there's another room you need to show me?" *Please, no.*

Dottie shook her head. "The only other rooms on this floor are Arnie's office and my sewing room. Bird free. Arnie's insistence." A narrowing of the eyes.

Arnie had been gone a long time, but Margo didn't point this out. If Dottie wanted to respect her late husband's wishes, she wasn't about to argue.

Margo walked back into the dining room and then the living room, taking notes and asking Dottie a few questions to understand her vision and offer a few suggestions of her own. In the end, they decided on pale yellow walls to brighten the space, with white furnishings, a new mirror above the mantle, and fresh throw pillows to offset colors in a rug that would be decided on together.

"These framed prints of the birds would still work well in here," Margo said, noticing the colors. "It's all about finding balance."

"Oh, thank you. When I saw your portfolio online, I just knew you'd be able to help me."

Margo raised an eyebrow. Had Dottie been snooping on her or simply shopping for a designer?

She decided not to think about that one too much.

"How long will something like this take?"

"If we can get the work started right away, only a few weeks," Margo said. "The worst part will be lining up the contractors to remove the wallpaper and then paint. I know the furniture store in town always has good pieces in stock."

"Oh, my nephew is a contractor," Dottie said. "He can handle the wallpaper removal and the painting."

"Perfect! If he can start right away, we can probably have this all done in about two weeks then."

A familiar look took over Dottie's features, one she got when she was keen for information she would stow away to dish out later. "And will you be able to stay in town for that long, or will your husband be needing you back?"

A two-week project. Was this a test? Dottie's way of fishing for gossip? From the gleam in her eye it was entirely possible.

Margo hesitated, knowing there was nothing to consider. Her life with Ash was over, and the sooner she accepted that the easier it would be to move on with her life.

She took a deep breath, only fleetingly wondering if she cared about the gossip mill, and said, "I'd love to take the project. I'll get started right away."

*

Margo was smiling a she walked away from Dottie's house, already dreaming up color schemes for the linens in the dining room and hoping that Dottie would agree to plantation shutters for the front room; they were costly, but it would give her just the amount of privacy she craved without losing any light. That sewing room would be a perfect place for the birds, tucked away at the back of the house, but somewhere that Dottie could sit and admire them.

She decided to stop by Bridget's office instead of calling her—she had to sign the lease for the next two weeks on the cottage anyway, and hope that no one else had already taken it first.

The real estate office was right on Main Street, with a

black front door flanked by two boxwood topiaries. Inside, an empty receptionist desk opened to a hallway, at the end of which a brass nameplate hung next to a closed door.

Margo knocked, hoping she wasn't interrupting an important meeting, but a few moments later, Bridget opened the door. It was immediately obvious that something was bothering her—her eyes had a red tinge at the edges and her lipstick was swiped off. The dark blond hair she usually kept neatly brushed at her shoulders was tied back in a loose ponytail that was coming undone at the sides.

"Sorry to stop by without calling first," Margo said, feeling out of place and a bit unwelcome.

"Don't worry about it," Bridget said, walking back to her desk and dropping into her chair.

"I actually came for professional reasons," Margo continued, thinking from the bleary look in her sister's face that yes, she really should have called first. "I wanted to take the cottage for another two weeks." When Bridget didn't immediately reply, Margo's heart skipped a beat. "If it's still available."

"It is," Bridget said slowly. She seemed to frown. "Another two weeks. You sure?"

No, she wasn't sure, not entirely, but she didn't see much alternative either. She'd been here for a week, and in that time she still hadn't heard from Ash, and she hadn't reached out to him either. She didn't know what to say. What to do. If there even was anything to say or do. It was easier to stay put.

"I—" She opened her mouth to tell Bridget how she was feeling, how she almost couldn't believe this was her life, that she stayed awake some nights feeling like this was all some bad dream and she would wake up from it in the morning. Other times, she wrestled with the possibility that it was all some misunderstanding. After all, this was Ash. Ash the homebody. Ash who frequented the same three restaurants and always ordered the same dish. Ash who was so predictable, she could tell you which tie he wore with which suit, because he never mixed and matched. Ash liked to sit at home and read or watch television, or play golf. Ash was quiet and bookish and he never even seemed to notice a particularly attractive waitress, for example.

But then, when was the last time he'd told her that she was attractive? When was the last time she'd made a special effort, worn a new dress, or added a touch of blush, and he'd noticed?

"Oh for God's sake!" Bridget scowled at her computer screen. "I completely forgot that tonight is my teacher conference! I was planning to take this couple out to look at starter homes, and now I'll have to reschedule."

"Can…Ryan go?" Margo wasn't sure if she should have even asked.

"He'll have an excuse. The bar never closes, after all." Bridget gave a heavy sigh and then sank her head into her hands. "Sometimes I just feel like it's all piling up. One thing after another. Like I can't handle it all on my own."

Margo bit her lip. Bridget didn't often appear flustered or overwhelmed. Stressed, yes, but always in control. Margo could only assume that there was a lot more going on than just a forgotten teacher conference.

"I'm sure the couple will understand. Or maybe Jeffrey could go in your place?"

Bridget shook her head. "No, it's fine. I'll figure out."

Margo paused, watching as Bridget seemed to hold in tears as she typed something on her keyboard. "I'm all ears if you want to unload."

Bridget stopped typing, then shook her head. "It's nothing. I'm overreacting. I'm tired is all." And with that, her mouth pinched tight, her chin lifted, and any hint of tears vanished.

She did seem tired, and out of sorts, but Margo knew her sister, and she knew when she was lying, or hiding something. Unlike Margo, who became all red in the face, Bridget simply shut down.

"Well, I have some errands to run," Margo said, sensing that Bridget needed to be alone to deal with things.

Bridget stopped typing again. "You were starting to tell me something?"

Margo hesitated. The moment had passed. She brushed a hand through the air more casually than she felt by the pressure in her chest. "I've taken on an assignment to redo some of Dottie's house."

"Dottie Joyce?" Bridget gaped.

As if there were another Dottie in this town. "She approached me and she…needs help." That was putting it mildly. Margo felt her smile return.

Bridget looked incredulous. "Huh. So you'll do it?"

"It pays well and it won't take long." Margo shrugged. If she kept talking she'd get into the heart of the matter, and Bridget's eyes were already drifting back to the computer screen. She wasn't up for it today. "So long as the cottage is available, I'll take it."

Bridget didn't question her decision further, and Margo took that as reinforcement that she shouldn't burden her sister with her problems just now. Clearly, Bridget had enough to deal with at the moment.

She walked down Main Street, stopping in the shops, checking out the window display in the furnishing store, and making a few mental notes for when she got started on her sketches tonight. Dottie's home was traditional, and given her passion for the historical society and the comings and goings of the town, she hoped to find some old maps of Oyster Bay, perhaps some artwork or ceramics made by a local artist that Dottie might feel a connection to. She was sentimental, Margo realized, and she certainly had a soft side. If Margo didn't know any better, she might think all that gossiping was a cover for Dottie's insecurities about herself. She might feel confident reporting the private lives of others, but from what Margo had observed, Dottie seemed very uncertain about her own.

Well, all the more reason she needed help. If Dottie felt comfortable letting people inside her home, she might feel better letting them into her life, which might help make her far less curious about everyone else.

The air was cold and she buttoned her borrowed coat, but the bare feet didn't help much. Two more weeks in Oyster Bay. She'd buy some staples.

Her favorite clothing shop in town was just ahead on the corner, and Margo hurried her step, grateful for the warmth when she door closed behind her. She walked to a table lined with sweaters, and had just picked up a grey crewneck when she felt a tap on her shoulder.

"Eddie!" She was sure her face registered a dozen emotions at once: surprise, fear, happiness, confusion. To name a few.

"I'm glad I ran into you. I've been wanting to talk to you, actually."

"Oh?" Her cheeks were turning warm, and she doubted it had anything to do with the heat in the store. It was the way he was looking at her, his eyes deep-set and unwavering and far too intense.

"I'm sorry if I upset you at the festival," Eddie said.

Margo smiled. "You didn't upset me. It's just been a confusing time for me."

"Would a hot meal cheer you up?" Eddie asked, and Margo nearly dropped the sweater she was holding. Was he asking her out on a date? "Just as friends," he clarified, to her mix of relief and disappointment. "What do you say? Tomorrow night? I'll do the shopping, don't worry."

"Wait. You mean, you're cooking?" She couldn't help but laugh.

"That so hard to believe?" His grin widened. "I'll come over. All you have to do is kick back and relax."

Margo was still skeptical. "Well, you certainly have evolved since the last time I saw you."

"More than you know," he said, his eyes losing their amusement.

Margo shifted on her feet, feeling uneasy. It was easier to hold onto the memory of a boy who had broken her heart instead of allowing herself to think that all the good parts of Eddie were still there, and that he'd grown older, wiser. Better.

"It's just dinner," he said with a shrug. "And I promise not to poison you."

Well, when he put it that way... "What are you making?"

He grinned. "I'll take that as a yes, and as for what I'm making, it's a surprise. But you'll like it."

"How do you know I'll like it?" She looked at him quizzically.

"Because I know you," he said, before turning toward the door.

He did know her. Inside and out. Even now after all these years. There were gaps, stories that could be filled in, experiences that could be shared, but the core of her, the heart of her…had always been a part of him, hadn't it?

"Eight o'clock?" He was watching her.

"Eight o'clock," she said, blinking rapidly. "I'm at the white cottage on Sea Glass Lane."

"I know," Eddie said with a grin. "Dottie told me."

Margo stood in the store, holding her bag, staring at the door as Eddie disappeared onto the sidewalk.

She set the sweater back on the table and walked over to the blouses hanging on the wall.

If she was having dinner with Eddie, she might need to buy more than just a sensible pair of shoes.

Chapter Twelve

Even though his shift ended at four on Wednesdays, Eddie usually stuck around for a bit, sharing some laughs with Sylvia or pushing paperwork, avoiding the inevitable return to his empty apartment and the thoughts that tended to encroach when he got there. The ones that said he had no excuse not to be at Serenity Hills right now instead.

But tonight, Eddie had legitimate plans. He pushed through the doors of The Corner Market, Oyster Bay's gourmet grocer in the heart of the town center. Usually the striped awning, piped café music, and outdoor flower stand intimidated him—besides, regardless of what he'd told Margo, most of his meals came from the pizza joint down the street or the take and bake section of the nearest Hannaford.

He grunted as he grabbed a cart, telling himself he'd be in and out in ten minutes. Fifteen, tops. He glanced over his shoulder as he approached the cheese display, which was set up like a French food stall, right down to the chalkboard sign that listed this week's special varieties.

If Sylvia caught wind of this, she'd never let him forget it.

He took the first cheese his hand touched, then, with another glance out the window, took a moment to consider his options. Brie. Gruyere. Some things he couldn't pronounce. He read a few of the flowery descriptions, smiling to himself, even though they did help him, loath as he was to admit it.

Next he moved onto the produce section where he quickly found some grapes to go with the cheese, and ingredients for a salad. All that was left was the fish and the dessert. See, this wasn't really a big deal at all.

"Eddie?"

He turned, hoping it wasn't Sylvia, even though rationally he knew that it wasn't her voice. Sylvia's voice was more of a growl. Husky and deep and just threatening enough to keep her looking tough for her job—and her kids.

"Aunt Lori." He exhaled in relief.

She laughed. "I don't bite."

"Sorry, just startled." He grinned. "I'm a little out of my element here."

"What's the occasion?" Lori looked down to inspect

his cart, and then gave him a suggestive look. "A date?"

"No." Not really, at least. "Just…dinner."

"Seems like a date to me!" Lori laughed when Eddie frowned and reached over to playfully swat his arm. "Don't mind me, it's none of my business. But don't be mad at me for getting my hopes up a bit."

"Your hopes?" Was she really that desperate to marry him off?

"Oh, you know…I guess I thought that if you found a nice girl in town, you might settle down here. I've liked having you back in Oyster Bay. And believe it or not, so has Steve."

Eddie wasn't so sure about that. After all, wasn't it his Uncle Steve that refused to take him back in all those years ago? "It's okay, Lori. You don't need to try to make me feel better. I know that I let you guys down all those years ago."

Lori looked surprised, and then hurt. "More like we felt we let *you* down. Steve sent you away to straighten you out, to help you. That's all we ever wanted for you."

Eddie pulled in a breath. Tough love. He understood. He'd practiced it himself in recent years.

"We'd always hoped you'd come back to town. And now…well, here you are." She smiled.

"Here I am." Eddie swallowed hard. Mick had emailed that afternoon, with more details of the job. It was everything that Eddie could have dreamed of and more. The chance to really do some good. To set up programs, clean up the streets, make a name for himself. Rewrite history.

"I hope she enjoys it, whoever she is." Lori wiggled her eyebrows, and Eddie managed a grin.

"I hope so, too." Not that he expected anything to come from it. Margo was still a married woman, and he wasn't exactly sure of his future himself.

"Will you come by for dinner next week?" Lori said, moving past him to inspect some apples, which looked as if they'd been brought in straight from the orchard that day.

"I'd like that," he agreed, and he would, very much. Those dinners with Lori, Steve, and Nick were the only family meals he'd ever had, then and even now. How many times after he'd gone back to Jersey, eating bologna sandwiches or bowls of cereal, alone in the trailer, did he dream about Lori's roast chicken and mashed potatoes and hot apple crisp for dessert? And even when he moved on, grew up, joined the force, his only hot meals still came from the microwave or a restaurant. But it wasn't just the food. It was the laughter, the warmth. Simple things like the way Lori always asked how his day was, and the way she genuinely seemed to care how he answered. His first Christmas in Oyster Bay had been one of the first real Christmases he'd ever had. His dad never did the whole tree and presents thing, and there definitely wasn't any Santa stopping by to save the day. But Lori made it special. She made everything special.

Just like Margo had, he thought, remembering that

first holiday and the ornament she'd given him as a gift. He'd kept it, all these years, even though he never had a tree to hang it on. He set it on his dresser instead, so it was the first thing he saw in the morning. And eventually, he took it down. Took every memory of this town and the life that was so different from his out of his mind. But try as he might, he could never take it out of his heart.

Sure, Mick had invited him over for the holidays every year, let him catch a glimpse of the whole suburban thing—a dog, two kids, a wife who called him "honey." As much as Eddie appreciated it, he couldn't wait to leave, to get back to the city, to his apartment, where he didn't have to think about all the things he might have wanted to have and couldn't seem to find.

Dating wasn't a problem, but he never got close. It was easier to keep to himself, be his own man, not worry about judgment or understanding or...good-byes.

He continued his shopping, even faster than planned, trying not to think about Mick's email or his life in Philly or all the people he might soon leave behind. Again.

*

Margo looked around the cottage, even though there was nothing to really worry about. She didn't need to straighten up—the furnishings were sparse. She'd lit a fire in the fireplace an hour ago, something she never got to do in Charleston because Ash didn't like the way it made the house smell, and now thought the better of it. It might send Eddie the wrong idea, that she thought this night was going to be something more than what it could be.

Even if maybe a part of her wished that it could.

She pulled in a sigh as she walked into the kitchen and took a bottle of sparkling water from the fridge. She selected two glasses and set them out on a tray, which she carried into the living room and set on the slipcovered ottoman. It was dark outside, but she could hear the waves crashing through the tall windows. The sound of the sea had a way of calming her; it always had. And tonight, she needed it.

She was nervous, and why shouldn't she be? She hadn't been alone with Eddie in more than a dozen years. Once it had felt so natural, so normal. Now...she feared long pauses and awkward silences. She feared having nothing to talk about. She feared having too much to talk about, connecting in a way that she hadn't connected in a long, long time.

There was a knock at the door. Oh, God. She set a hand to her stomach, which was knotting and fluttering all at once, and smoothed her sweater over her hips to collect herself. She walked to the door, took a deep breath in and out, and then opened it to see Eddie standing there, holding up two paper bags from The Corner Market, a big grin on his face.

And...she swooned. Just a little.

"Cute place," he said as he pushed past her. He slipped off his shoes, took a look around, and managed to find his own way to the kitchen. He deposited the bags on the counter and shrugged out of his coat, which he hung over the back of a barstool.

He was making this easy for her. Too easy. It was as if no time had passed. As if this were just another night, as if these dinners were a regular occurrence.

She suddenly wished they could be.

"What's on the menu?" she asked, feeling her shoulders relax. He'd pushed up his sweater sleeves and she watched his forearms flex as he pulled the items from the bag. Her stomach dipped and soared. She looked away. Busied herself with finding a cutting board for the cheese and crackers.

"Salmon with a roasted vegetable salad and a surprise for dessert."

"It isn't every day I get a meal from The Corner Market," she said, grinning as he unwrapped the cheese and opened the boxes of crackers.

"Me either," he admitted, and Margo felt her pulse skip, realizing he'd made a special effort.

"How's this for a salmon?"Eddie grinned as he set a huge filet wrapped in paper down on the cutting board.

"Delicious. Can I help?"

"No." Eddie shook his head. "I invited you to dinner, this is all on me. You just sit and relax and look pretty."

Silence. Margo felt her cheeks flush as Eddie opened a few cupboards and eventually found what he needed to bake the fish.

"What about the salad—" she started, noticing the

ingredients, but a sharp look from Eddie made her laugh. "I didn't know you knew how to cook."

He paused. "Confession. This is one of only two meals I know how to cook, and I learned from some dude on that television channel."

Now Margo was really laughing, all thoughts of his comment about her being pretty forgotten. Well, almost. "So what do you do for dinner most nights?"

"Pizza." He grinned. "Microwavable meals? Sometimes I go over to my Uncle Steve and Aunt Lori's." He added some seasoning to the filet of salmon.

"And back in Philly?" She was eager for information, about his life there, about everything she had missed all these years.

"Oh, the same. Maybe a cheese steak for variety." He winked, and God help her, her stomach fluttered. "It was just me and Dad for a while, and then it was just me. I had to figure out how to make something, or I wouldn't eat."

Margo frowned. She didn't like thinking of Eddie living that way. It was easier to think of him at Steve and Lori Boyd's house, the cute cedar-shingled Colonial with the white shutters.

"How is your dad?" she asked.

Eddie said nothing as he preheated the oven and moved on to the salad. "Not well. I don't visit very often. It's..." He seemed to struggle for the right word and finally said, "Complicated."

"I'm sure. But you must be on better terms now…if you're here?"

Eddie looked over the counter at her, square in the eye. "I didn't come back for my father. I came back for Uncle Steve and Aunt Lori. They were good to me. And they asked me to come."

"But your father surely wants you here too," Margo protested.

Eddie looked back down at the vegetables he'd set out on a cutting board. "Pretty convenient, huh? He wasn't there when I needed him, and now…" He shook his head.

Margo saw the hurt flash in his eyes, just like when they were younger, when the kids at school would tease. "You're a good man, Eddie." She swallowed hard, realizing it was true.

She waited until he had the salmon in the oven and timer set before saying, "I have some sparkling water for us in the living room. Maybe we could start with the cheese?"

They walked into the main room, where Margo studied the furniture arrangement. Should she sit next to him, on the one sofa, or take an armchair instead? It would make for an awkward reach for the ottoman, though.

Eddie solved the problem for her by taking a spot on the floor, the fireplace at his back. She grinned and did the same, opposite him, her back against the sofa.

"How do you like being back in Oyster Bay?" he asked.

She pulled in a breath. "I don't know. At first, it felt strange, but now...now it will be hard to think about leaving again." And what would she do? Go back to Ash? Or just go back to South Carolina? To her nail salon and French restaurant and rolodex of clients...That didn't seem like her life at all anymore. She had friends, but they were more like acquaintances. "I'd miss my sisters," she said.

He frowned. "Are you planning on going back to Charleston?"

Margo didn't immediately reply. "I don't know what I'm doing," she finally said. "My entire life is there, at least that's what I thought, but being back here with my sisters, and even Mimi, well, it reminds me of how much I left behind."

"And your husband?"

Margo snapped a cracker in half, enjoying the satisfaction of the sound it made. "My husband cheated on me. And I have to figure out how to move forward."

He nodded, but didn't push for further details. "You'll figure it out. Big decisions take time."

"So do big changes," she said, raising her eyebrows.

"I was offered a job in Philly," Eddie blurted. "With my old partner. A good opportunity. One I wouldn't have expected."

"Oh." Her mouth felt dry. Of course. She should have known. Eddie was only in Oyster Bay because of his father, and soon, he'd have no reason to stay. "Did you make a decision?"

"I have to give him one by this Friday."

This Friday. It seemed so sudden. He was only just now back in her life. How could he be gone again so quickly?

She wanted to ask him to stay. To do things different this time. But she couldn't. She was a married woman, technically. Her house, her belongings, her life was across the country. How could she ask him to stay in Oyster Bay when she wasn't even so sure she'd be staying here herself?

"It's a good opportunity. A chance to make a difference. It's one of the things I like about being an officer, I get to help people; even if it's only for a day, it's something." He paused. "There was a boy I knew. Jesse. He had a bad home life and didn't have anyone to help him make better decisions. He didn't have a future. I brought him in a few times, petty crimes, and then one day I cut him a deal. If he played it straight, I'd help him out. Get him into a few after school programs, that sort of thing."

Margo stared at him. "That's really wonderful, Eddie."

"He lasted a few months and then disappeared. Right back to where he started. Or worse." Eddie looked down. "I have no idea."

She reached over to hold his hand, and then thought better of it, and reached for her glass instead. "You did your best, Eddie. That's all you could do."

"But I tried to help him. I wanted to save him!"

Margo gave a sad smile. My, that sounded familiar. "You can't save everyone. They have to do it on their own."

Just like Eddie had, she thought. He went from being an angry, lonely kid, to a strong, confident man who knew who he was and wasn't ashamed of where he'd come from. He'd fought against his circumstances, reached for something better.

Gone was the boy who sat alone at lunch until the day she'd joined him at the table, under the guise of finding a partner for a school assignment.

"Do you remember that time we worked on that English paper together?" It was the beginning of their friendship. She never could have known then where it would lead them.

He seemed to perk up as he searched for the memory. "*Catcher in the Rye*. We must have sat at Angie's Café for six hours writing that paper!"

"She just kept refilling our coffee." Margo smiled. They were too young to be drinking coffee, but they were also too young to admit that to each other. Looking back, they each had their insecurities. He had a reputation. And she…well, she had a crush.

"You know, I kept that book. It has all your notes in the margin."

Her heart swelled. "I'd love to see that sometime."

"Gladly. After all, I got an A. It was the first A I'd ever gotten." He grinned, and oh, she clung to that look, all boyish and sweet and full of so many feel good memories.

"But not the last," Margo pointed out. "You would have gotten more if you didn't keep cutting class."

His expression darkened, and Margo wished she hadn't let the mood dip. "Wouldn't have had to cut if things had been easier." Now he grinned, that same wicked grin he'd give her when he picked her up on that old dusty motorcycle that had once belonged to his Uncle Steve. "Besides, I was always outside the school gates at three, waiting for you."

"That you were," she said. "I could always count on that."

"And I could always count on you," he said, his voice low and husky.

Her heart was beating fast in her chest as she watched him slide around the ottoman until he was sitting beside her, so close she could feel the heat of his body, smell the musk of his shampoo. So close that if she closed her eyes it would be like no time had passed, and they were just Margo and Eddie. How it used to be. How it should have been.

"I want to kiss you right now," he said, and Margo felt her heart speed up. A hundred thoughts seem to whirr through her mind all at once. Thoughts of kissing Eddie on the beach when they were just teenagers. The first, glorious, tentative kiss under the tree in Bent Park. The last, slow, tear-filled kiss on her front stoop. And Ash.

But she didn't think of Ash kissing her. She thought of Ash kissing that other woman.

She wanted Eddie to kiss her, just like a part of her had wanted him to kiss her the other day at the festival. She wanted to go back to that time and place where everything in the world was right. When a kiss was soft and sweet and straight from the heart. To a moment when she felt loved, and wanted. She wanted Eddie to kiss her. Then, now, maybe, in her heart, always. She licked her bottom lip, preparing her response, even though she wasn't sure what it would be, but before she could say anything, he said, "But I'm not going to."

Oh. Well there went that dilemma. She wondered if the disappointment registered on her face. She should be relieved, really. It would make her life more complicated than it already was. And a kiss from Eddie was...complicated.

"I hope that doesn't mean dessert is off the table, though," he said, giving her a slow grin that she couldn't resist.

She couldn't be mad at Eddie. He was making the right choice for both of them. He was being the adult. The responsible one. She grinned at the thought.

The timer on the oven went off, pulling her from this moment and back to reality.

"Only if it's chocolate," she said, standing to follow him into the kitchen.

Chapter Thirteen

By Friday morning, Bridget knew that there was no more avoiding it: she'd have to accept Ian Fowler's best and final offer on the house.

She stared at the framed photo on her desk, taken last Christmas in front of the small, fake tree she'd been setting up every year since she and Ryan had separated. Every year she told herself that this would be the last year, that next year she'd have money for a real tree to fill a bigger space. That she'd have a backyard where Emma could build snowmen. A chimney that Santa could come down, not the slightly creepy story she spun to her daughter about Santa having a magical key to their front door. Bridget could feel Emma's childhood ticking away. It wouldn't be too long before she didn't have interest in a tree swing or even those coveted piano lessons. She told herself that all she needed were a few big sales...and now she had one. The biggest listing of her career. And she couldn't even enjoy it.

Sighing, she picked up the phone and dialed the number of Ian Fowler. He answered on the third ring, just when she'd started to almost hope he'd changed his mind.

Nonsense. She couldn't afford for him to change his mind. And it wouldn't do Mimi any good either.

"So, do I have the house?" he asked.

Did he have to be so literal about it? Couldn't he have just said something to the effect of, *Do we have a deal?*

"As you know, I represent the seller of this house as well," she began. Just say it, she told herself. Accept the offer. Accept reality. She'd accepted the reality of her marriage with Ryan, after all. Made the heart-wrenching and difficult decision to move on, to hope for something better. Why should this be any more difficult?

"And the house is unoccupied at this time?"

"Yes," Bridget said sadly. It was hard to think of that big old house sitting alone. It was a family house, meant to be filled with love and laughter. Ian and his undoubtedly gorgeous fiancée would probably have a backyard wedding this spring and fill the house with beautiful offspring by the following year. Bridget knew she should be happy about this.

"Good. I'd like to move the closing up by thirty days," Ian said.

Before Thanksgiving, Bridget calculated. Her throat felt scratchy when she said, "I don't see that being a problem." They'd have an estate sale, sell as much as they could, keep only the most sentimental of items. It would be the best time to do it, after all. Margo was in town, and they could fairly divide the items. Margo would want the wedding dishes of course, and really, who was Bridget to stop her? The only thing Bridget wanted from that house was the house itself. And the piano, she thought, with a frown.

"Great," Ian was saying. "I want to get my men in there before the holidays."

"Men?" Bridget frowned.

"Contractors," Ian clarified.

"Oh." Bridget's heart was racing. "So you decided to bring down that wall in the front room then?" What a shame. Those bookshelves were always filled with framed photos and Mimi's Hummel figurines.

"No, this is a full gut," Ian said, and if Bridget didn't know better, she might think he was chuckling.

A full gut. She blinked rapidly at her desk, unable to speak.

"Best thing about the place is the land, as I'm sure you'll agree."

Bridget couldn't agree, but she couldn't slam the phone down either. She paused, mentally replaying their conversation, knowing she hadn't yet agreed to the final offer he'd emailed her with that morning. "As I said at the start of the call, I represent the seller as well, and..."

Her mind was spinning. "And the seller would like the weekend to consider the final offer."

"So, Monday?" Ian didn't sound pleased, but Bridget couldn't worry about that now.

"Monday," she confirmed, letting her gaze drift back to the picture of Emma.

She had the weekend to hold on to hope. Or denial.

Or the part of her past that she just couldn't seem to let go of.

*

Margo had grown used to her daily walks into town, and today was no exception. Leaves of orange and crimson gathered at the base of white picket fences that lined the sidewalk and crunched under her ballet flats as she followed the familiar path, slowing her pace every now and again to admire the pumpkins on people's doorstops, or a new wreath someone had hung on a door.

Fall was her favorite time of the year, and she'd missed the full experience living so far south. She drew a big breath of crisp autumn air and grinned. Fall always had a way of stirring up optimism in her, and even as an adult, she couldn't help but live by the school calendar, partially due to the fact that she had married a professor. Fall was the time for new beginnings, and maybe, just maybe, she'd found her new fresh start here, in a place that wasn't new to her at all.

She walked past The Corner Market, stopping to

admire the potted mums and fat pumpkins that were for sale outside the door. She glanced in the window, thinking of Eddie walking the aisles, selecting the ingredients for their dinner. She thought of the grin on his face when she'd opened the door and he held up the bags and her heart had turned over. And then she thought of the way he'd looked later, when they said good-bye, and he lingered in the doorway, as if he might just kiss her after all.

But he hadn't. And that was for the best.

Or so she kept telling herself.

She hadn't heard from him since dinner the other night, but Oyster Bay was small, and the weekend was coming up. For now she was happy to keep busy with plans for Dottie's redesign. It was the perfect distraction. From a lot of things.

The Lantern was up ahead now, and Margo quickened her pace so she wasn't late to meet her sister. Bridget had called an hour ago, asking if Margo could meet her for lunch, and Margo had happily set aside her plans for Dottie's living room to do so, even if she did have a funny feeling this lunch was more than a social call.

Her sister had been selectively quiet about her showing with the big client from New York. She was keeping something from Margo, no doubt. Something that might now be revealed.

Bridget was sitting at a table of the restaurant when Margo walked in, grateful for the warmth and the touch of classical music playing in the background. She looked around the room for a sign of Chip, but other than a young waitress in the signature black shirt and skirt that constituted a uniform, the place was full of customers only.

She barely had a chance to drape her coat over the chair when she saw Bridget's wan smile and felt her own slip. "You don't look so good."

"You've never looked better," Bridget replied.

Margo felt her cheeks flush. Was it really that obvious?

"Margo." Bridget hesitated. "What's going on? I mean, why are you really back in Oyster Bay? Is everything okay between you and Ash?"

Margo frowned. She didn't like thinking about Ash, not when she'd woke up in such a good mood, not just because of her night with Eddie, but because of the prospect of growing her business, right here in Oyster Bay, and the thought of lunch with her sister—a warm bowl of chowder on a crisp, fall day.

"Ash has been fooling around behind my back." Now that it was out there, it couldn't be taken back. Her husband had lied and cheated. Her family knew.

"I never liked that guy," Bridget said, scowling.

"What?" This was news to Margo. Just recently Bridget had claimed that Margo knew how to pick 'em.

"I mean, look, don't get me wrong. He seemed stable and responsible. You didn't have to worry about things like him losing his job or forgetting to pay the mortgage or—" She stopped herself and looked down at her water glass.

"Or cheat on me? Or leave me?" Margo's chest felt heavy. "I know. I thought the same thing."

"He had qualities, at first glance," Bridget said. "Ones I thought could make up for his shortcomings."

"His shortcomings?" Margo frowned and waited for her sister to continue.

"Don't you remember your wedding? How you had to do whatever his mother wanted, without any say of your own? You wanted tulips for your flowers, and you had roses, for example. Peach roses, because Nadine liked peach. And you had to go with the lemon cake because it was Reynolds family tradition, even though you wanted vanilla."

Margo hadn't thought about that in a long time. Maybe she hadn't let herself. "It wasn't important," she said, but that wasn't true. She'd been upset about the peach roses. She'd wanted the tulips, and if she had to have roses, she wanted white ones. But Nadine had already ordered her dress, which was, of course, peach, and she'd made such a stink that Ash had begged her to just go along with it, claiming they were just flowers, and Margo had felt petty for causing a stink.

"It *was* important," Bridget said. "And you went along with it because Ash insisted and you didn't want to ruffle feathers. He didn't put you first, and you deserve to be put first."

Margo knew that her sister had a point. There were countless examples, little things, that could have added up over time if she'd let them, like the way Ash always decided how they spent their weekends, and the way Margo never disagreed, because she didn't want an argument.

"Can I ask you something?" Bridget said. "When was the last time you really laughed with Ash?"

Margo tried to think of a recent time and came up blank. "We don't have a relationship like that."

Bridget tipped her head. "Don't you think you should?"

Margo felt her stomach tighten. Of course she should, but it wasn't always that easy. You could fall in love, have all the butterflies and flutters that came with it, all the joy and laughter, and then...Then it could all be gone. The way it had all gone away when Eddie left.

All the good feelings about Eddie were suddenly replaced with bad ones, memories of the way she'd felt when he disappeared, without explanation, and the loss of that happiness they'd once shared was gone forever.

The loss of Ash was different. Not easier, but somehow less painful.

"I always did want a wedding at the house," Margo said sadly.

"Me too. Instead, I eloped because deep down I was afraid Ryan would get cold feet with a long engagement. And now it's too late for a big, backyard wedding." Bridget looked miserable. "I got an offer on the house. A good offer. I don't see how I can refuse to accept it. Mimi put me in charge of this, and we need the money to pay for the nursing home. I have to set my emotions aside, but...I'm struggling."

Margo's breath was still. Of course. It was just a matter of time. And it wasn't her home, not anymore. It hadn't been in a long, long time.

So why did it suddenly feel like she'd never left? That everything she'd ever wanted had been right here all along? And that somehow it could all slip away again...

Chapter Fourteen

There was a strange car parked behind hers when Margo arrived at the cottage two hours later, her heart heavy, her tread a little slower than usual. She stopped, wondering if the landlord had stopped by, or another real estate agent from the office, needing more paperwork signed.

But then she saw him, sitting on the front stoop, in jeans and a dress shirt, looking every damn bit as remorseful as he should.

Every damn bit as guilty as he was.

"Ash."

She forced herself forward, even though her heart was pounding. From anger, from hurt, she didn't know anymore.

"How'd you find me?" she asked, stopping a good four feet from where he stood. *And why'd it take so long?*

She grew angry at the thought.

"It wasn't hard to figure out you'd be back in Oyster Bay," he replied. "I stopped for a coffee in town and ran into some woman named Dottie. She told me where you were staying." He paused, then jutted his chin to the door. "Can we talk?"

Margo blew out a breath and nodded. It was inevitable. The conversation needed to be had and today, she was ready to have it.

He stood, but she sidestepped him toward the door, her hands shaking as she pushed the key into the hole and turned it. If he had any comments about why she was staying here and not at the house, he didn't ask. Perhaps Dottie had already filled him in on that too.

Margo hung up her coat, noticing that Ash, being unprepared for the weather, wasn't wearing one. She knew she could ask him to sit down, offer him a glass of water or some food, but she wasn't in the mood to make this easy for him, and besides, he wasn't her guest. She hadn't invited him here, and, she realized, she didn't want him here. This was her world. Her town. Her family. Her friends. Her past.

Her life.

"So I guess you know…" He combed a hand through his hair, looking at her sheepishly.

Margo waited a beat. "Know what exactly? About you and your grad student?"

"It's not what you think," Ash said, but he stopped when he saw the sharp look she gave him.

"Not what I think?" Had he rehearsed this line from some bad movie? "I don't see what else it could be, Ash, but if you have an explanation, I'm all ears."

"She...she likes me, Margo."

She nodded, her lids drooping. She wasn't buying it.

"And I'm not going to lie, it felt good to be...wanted."

She scowled at him. "What's that supposed to mean?"

"I think you know damn straight what it means. You and I—we were never like that. Maybe at first, but then..."

Margo swallowed the lump that was building in her throat. She knew what he meant. She'd known it herself. The only difference was that maybe she hadn't seen it as soon as he did. Instead, she had fooled herself into thinking everything was fine.

"That doesn't mean I can just forgive you for cheating on me. You lied to me."

"I don't expect you to forgive me." Ash's face was lined, his eyes had a sad look to them, and Margo couldn't overlook the fact that he hadn't corrected her. That it was true. He had lied to her. Cheated on her.

"Why are you here?" she asked wearily. She wanted nothing more than to sit down. To drop onto the soft, slipcovered sofa and close her eyes. She suddenly felt exhausted. Like she could sleep straight through until morning.

Then it occurred to her that he might be here to ask for a divorce. She waited, her pulse quickening, the finality of everything closing in on her.

"Because I wanted to see you. Because I knew when I came home that day and you were gone that you'd seen…that you knew." He looked at her pleadingly. "Because I missed you."

Margo felt as if she'd been slapped. She took a step back, staring at this man, trying to figure out who he was and if she'd ever even known him at all. "You missed me?"

"I know you probably won't believe this now, but…I really missed you, Margo."

She shook her head. "No. No, what you missed was our life. Our routine."

"Maybe." He shrugged. "What's wrong with that?"

"A lot is wrong with that, as you were so quick to point out," she reminded him. "That comfortable domestic life you miss so much isn't enough for you."

And it wasn't enough for her either, she thought. Not anymore. Even if he hadn't cheated, the thought of going back to the life now made Margo feel empty, instead of comforted.

"But it's something," Ash said. "Something to build on."

"Build on?" She managed not to laugh. "You cheated on me, Ash." A part of her wanted to ask the hard questions, to know if it was the first time, to know if it was only one girl. But then the other half of her knew that it didn't even matter. It didn't change what he had done. It didn't change the way he felt.

Or the way she felt. Her marriage was over. She'd known it when she came to Oyster Bay and she knew it even more now.

"I want to try again. I want to try to make this work." His voice was firm, certain, even. But it wasn't convincing. "Ten years. It can't all be for nothing."

"It wasn't for nothing," Margo realized. And it hadn't been. There had been good times, moments of laughter and friendship and fondness, even love. Those years couldn't be erased any more than they could ever happen again.

The doorbell rang, and Margo frowned, wondering who was dropping by unannounced. Few people even knew where she was staying. If it was Bridget, Ash had better run, she thought, not bothering to warn him. She opened the door, her eyes widening when she saw Eddie on the stoop, his hands thrust into the pocket of his jeans, his grin wide and excited.

"Hey."

She swallowed. Her heart was pounding now. "Eddie."

The smile on his face fell when he looked over her shoulder. She didn't need to turn to know what he saw.

"I didn't realize I was interrupting," he said tightly.

"It's not what you think," she started to say, but right at that moment, Ash stepped forward and extended his hand.

"Ashley Reynolds," he said.

Eddie's gaze almost imperceptibly flitted to hers.

"Margo's husband," Ash added.

"Eddie Boyd. Old friend." His eyes were stony now.

Old friend. Not friend. The distinction was clear.

"Eddie," Margo protested, but his jaw was set.

"I was just stopping by to bring you this." He handed her a well-worn paperback. She didn't need to look at the cover to know the title. It was *The Catcher in the Rye*. He'd kept it, all these years, just as he'd said.

Her chest sagged. "Eddie."

He didn't meet her eye. "I'll see you, Margo." He turned, walked toward his car, not stopping or looking back. Margo watched him go, her heart hurting.

"Was that Eddie from juvie?" Ash asked, incredulous.

Margo was surprised that Ash would remember this bit of her past, but she refused to be touched by it. Ash may know her, but he certainly didn't understand her. Or care about her. Not really.

"That was a long time ago," Margo said defensively.

Ash's gaze was stony. "People don't change, Margo."

"You have," she said lightly. "Or maybe you were never the person I thought you were. Maybe I wanted you to be something you weren't."

The truth in that statement hit her hard.

"Don't do this, Margo." He stepped forward, taking her hand, and she let him, knowing it would be for the last time. "Let's try again. Let me try again. Please, Margo. Come home."

She held his hand, holding onto her past for one last moment, before letting it go. "I am home."

*

The old Eddie would have gone straight from Margo's to Dunley's for a beer, which would have turned into two, and then three. And then…nothing good ever happened then.

Eddie drove through town, past Dunley's and The Lantern. His shift didn't start for three hours, but the clock was ticking for a decision to Mick. He had half a mind to call him right now and tell him yes, he accepted, he'd go back to Philly, to a job that would challenge him, excite him, make him feel like he was making a difference. Like he had a purpose. After all, what argument could he really make for staying here in Oyster Bay? He'd left this town half a lifetime ago, and it had moved on. And so had he.

He kept driving, going nowhere in particular, wanting to keep going, all the way to Philly, and to not stop until he got there. But he'd done that before. Run from his problems. Made a pattern of it, really. A pattern he was determined to break.

Just before the road turned ahead was the entrance to Serenity Hills. Eddie eased off the gas, feeling his back teeth graze as they did every time he saw that sign. He drove past the entrance, followed the road's winding path instead, but every minute that passed made his chest feel heavier.

He couldn't escape it. No matter how hard he tried.

He could blame his dad for ruining his life. Or he

could blame himself.

At the next road he turned back, toward town, toward Serenity Hills. This time he pulled into the parking lot, got out of the car before he second-guessed himself, and went inside. The woman at the front desk barely looked up from her magazine when he signed himself in and walked down the hall, knowing there was no risk of running into Margo today.

His father's room was at the end of the hall, and the door was open, just like it always was. He hovered in the frame, looking at the frail man asleep in the bed. A man who used to seem so big and boorish, reduced now to skin and bones.

He rubbed a hand over his jaw and stepped inside. He hadn't looked around this room, not properly, at least. Usually when he came to visit Ray, it was for a brief stop, and he kept his eyes on the television, or out into the hallway. But today he took the chair next to the bed and stared at his father's face, straight on.

Ray's sleep was sound, he didn't stir, and Eddie studied his features. The nose they shared. The chin, too. Not much else, he thought grimly. Maybe just a handful of bad memories. But they were still memories. Someday soon that's all he'd have.

He didn't remember his mother—she'd left before those impressions could cement. But he'd seen her picture, buried deep in his father's bedside drawer, and he knew he looked like her. He never asked about her, he knew better, and the one and only time he did, Ray had made it clear he didn't know her whereabouts and wasn't going to share. They were never married. Ray wouldn't even tell Eddie her full name.

For years he wondered if this was why his father so often looked at him with contempt. Was he angry for being dumped with a kid? Or was he angry that his kid looked like her, a woman whose photo he still kept, all those years later.

"Eddie? Eddie Boyd?"

Eddie startled and turned to see Mrs. Harper, Margo's grandmother, sitting in her wheelchair, a large cat resting comfortably on her lap.

"Mrs. Harper." He went to stand, but she swatted her hand.

"I thought that was you. Did you come with my granddaughter?"

Eddie's mouth thinned. "No. I came alone."

"Ah, well, maybe one of them will visit later. It's hard, you know. Being here. Waiting. Sometimes I don't know what I'm waiting for anymore." Her eyes seemed to cloud. "You're all he talks about, you know."

Eddie frowned. "Excuse me?"

"Ray." Mimi pointed at his father as if to erase any confusion. "I stop in here now and again if Pudgie runs off." She stroked the animal fondly. "He loves visiting the residents, you know. Most people claim he's a little sunshine in their day."

Eddie grinned at the cat and went to pet it, but it

hissed so loudly at him that he jumped back.

Mimi grinned. "He's very protective of me."

"I can see that," Eddie remarked, waiting for his pulse to resume normal speed.

"Pudgie's fond of your father. Runs here a few times a week. So Ray and I got to talking once about how you used to date my granddaughter before she married that woman."

Eddie opened his mouth to correct her, until he saw the gleam in her eye.

"You know I'm just messing with her," Mimi said with a grin. "It gets boring in here. You've got to get your jollies somewhere. But don't go telling her I said that."

"I won't." Eddie pulled in a breath. He might not be telling Margo anything ever again. The thought of it saddened him, even though he had no rights to her. He'd let her go. Made his choice. A long, long time ago.

"Ray here boasts nonstop about you. His son, the cop. Asks me to tell him stories about you and Margo."

Eddie stared at Mrs. Harper in disbelief. "My father?"

"Of course your father! He looks forward to your visits, too. Gets a little nervous, even. Always careful to make a good impression. He'll be sorry he missed you today."

Ray let out a soft snore, and Eddie shook his head. "I didn't...I didn't realize."

"I don't know the man very well, but it's clear that he's made his share of mistakes. It takes a lot of courage to own up to that and try and make things right."

Eddie nodded. He hadn't thought of it that way. He'd been too busy holding onto anger and resentment. Things that could only ever hold you back, not move you forward.

"Thank you, Mrs. Harper. I appreciate you telling me that."

"I'll let Ray know you came by," Mimi said, as she wheeled herself out of the room.

"No," Eddie said, before he could even realize what he was saying. "I'll stay until he wakes up. I'll stay."

He turned to his father, watched the slow rise and fall of his chest, and knew in that moment that he couldn't leave him again. Even if his father had failed him, even if he'd left him when his son needed him the most, he was here now. The past was in the past. And in the past it would remain.

He pulled his phone from his pocket, taking a deep breath before pulling up Mick's number.

He could never change the past. But he could sure as hell change the future. Or, at least, try.

Chapter Fifteen

The next morning the sun shone bright in the clear blue sky, and for the first time in longer than she could remember, Margo woke with a feeling of possibility. She showered and dressed, knowing that today she would have to drive into town for some cold weather clothes. Ash was sending some of her things, and, eventually, she would go back to Charleston to collect the rest and divide their belongings, but not today. Today she needed to sit down, make a plan for herself, and start imagining the rest of her life—something she hadn't done since she was just a teenager.

She pulled her hair into a ponytail and set the brush down on the bathroom counter. Her diamond solitaire caught the light and sparkled back at her. Margo stared at her rings, which she had worn every day for most of her adult life, even recently, despite what had happened, and she knew that today it was time to take them off. She slid the engagement ring off first, thinking of how young and hopeful she'd been when she'd accepted it, how special she'd felt to wear the princess-cut diamond on the platinum band—how secure. Next she slid the wedding band off, the simple ring that had been a daily symbol of her commitment. And she had committed, hadn't she? She'd tried, as best she could. Maybe she could have tried harder. But maybe, deep down, she couldn't have. She'd given Ash all she could give him. And he'd done the same. And in the end, they'd admitted defeat.

She took the rings into the bedroom and set them in the drawer of the bedside table. Then, before she could think about how naked her hand felt, how the emptiness reminded her that something was missing, she grabbed her car keys and drove into town.

The Lantern was closed, but Chip would be there, of course, getting a start on the day before the lunch crowd hit. She parked her car behind his Jeep and walked around to the back screen door, relieved to see her uncle sitting at the bar instead of handling fish. She knocked to give him fair warning, and then let herself in.

"Margo!" Chip looked up, and at the sight of his grin, something shifted in Margo, and she burst into tears. "What's this about?" he asked in surprise, standing to put his arm around her.

"I don't know," she said. But she did know. It was the

smile. The warmth. The knowledge that this man was her family, someone who loved her, and that for as long as she'd stayed away, he was always here. It was the sense of loss, of time that could never be taken back. Of a life that hadn't worked out. A love that had faded and died. "I just…can't hold it in anymore."

"Come on," he said, guiding her onto a bar stool. "Have one on me."

At this, she laughed. It wasn't even nine o'clock yet. "Got any coffee?"

She wiped her eyes with the back of her hand as Chip poured them each a mug from the pot he had warming in the kitchen, but the tears were steady and warm on her cheeks.

Chip walked back into the room and handed her one of his sturdy white cotton napkins. "Creamers are in the bowl."

"I'm sorry," Margo said, as she continued to cry.

"Hey, this is what I'm here for." He gave her a wink as he set her mug down. "I figured you'd come talk to me when you were ready."

Margo wrapped her hands around the steaming mug. "Ash and I split up."

God, that sounded strange. So…permanent.

Chip didn't look surprised. "Figured it was something like that."

"Really?"

He cocked an eyebrow. "You come to town, without your husband, and you're renting a cottage. I hear you're decorating Dottie Joyce's house, too."

Margo didn't need to ask where he'd heard that bit of information.

"And you've been hanging around Eddie Boyd again."

"We're just friends," she said stiffly, recalling Eddie's words the day before. The hurt in his eyes when he turned to go. The way his smile fell when he looked over her shoulder. "And the fact that you know this is what I hate about this town. Everyone knows everything."

Chip shrugged. "Only because most of them care."

Margo frowned. She hadn't thought of it that way. "Ash was cheating on me. You know that too?"

"That bastard." Chip swore under his breath. "Need me to punch him for you?"

"It's tempting," Margo said with a little smile.

They lapsed into silence, sipping their coffee. Finally, Chip spoke. "Can I tell you something?"

She wasn't sure she had much of a choice. Or that she would like what he was about to say. She looked up. "Sure."

Chip seemed to hesitate. "The day you got married, your mother said to me, if you were even half as happy as she was, then that's all she could hope for."

The floodgates opened again. Tears flowers down her cheek, over her mouth, faster than she could wipe at them. "I don't talk about my parents much," she explained, when she was able to talk.

"I know," Chip said. "Sometimes I envied you.

Getting away. Not having to face the reminders. But it's nice to keep them alive, too. Every time I walk by the pier, I remember the time your mom and I raced to the edge, and she slipped and fell in. She must have been only ten. When I reached down to pull her up, she dragged me in with her." He laughed, then stopped abruptly. "I miss her." He looked suddenly so pained, that it was Margo's turn to dry her tears and set a hand on his wrist.

"Why do you think she said that, Chip? On my wedding day?" Margo looked at him carefully.

"Honestly? I think she was worried about you."

"She never let on to me!" Instead, she had fluffed her dress, handed her the bouquet, and told her she looked beautiful.

"It wouldn't have been fair of her." Chip glanced at her sidelong. "Sometimes we parents have to just watch and worry in silence."

"What was she worried about?" Margo asked, but she had a feeling she knew.

"I think…I think she wanted to be sure you were following your heart."

Margo nodded. Of course. She sipped her coffee, thinking about her mother, her years in that old house that would soon belong to someone else, and she thought of this town, and the people in it, and the memories that were all connected, all shared by so many, right here in Oyster Bay.

Her mother had been right to worry. Margo hadn't followed her heart. She had run from it.

Something she wouldn't do again.

"Thanks for the talk, Chip," she said, stepping down from the stool.

"You know where to find me," he said.

"Yes," she said with a smile. "I do."

She walked outside, into the sunshine, wishing she had her sunglasses to hide the redness in her eyes, but then she thought about what Chip had said. She couldn't run anymore. She couldn't hide. Her secrets would be exposed, but she was safe here. She was home.

"Margo!"

She turned to see Dottie coming toward her at a purposeful pace, suddenly doubting her sentimental feelings.

"Dottie! You'll have to excuse my allergies…" And now her eyes were flitting and her cheeks were burning. It was no use trying to deny the truth. She'd try to dodge it instead. "I was thinking we should turn your sewing room into a space for the birds. It's right off the kitchen and—"

"No." Dottie's tone was decisive. "I have a better idea. Let's put the birds in my husband's study. The room is bigger and the windows let in more light."

"Are you sure?" Margo asked. "I thought he wasn't fond of them."

"He wasn't. And that's why it's the perfect place for them." Dottie took Margo's elbow and leaned in close to whisper, "You may have heard the stories about him being lost at sea on a fishing trip."

A rather strange story, indeed, Margo had always thought.

"The truth of the matter is that he's been living in Albany for the past twenty-nine years with a woman named Joan."

Margo blinked. "I didn't know."

"I know you didn't know. I made sure no one knew. But I thought you might understand." She gave Margo a kind smile.

"I do understand," Margo replied, for once happy to confide in the woman.

Dottie patted her arm and then released it. "You'll be fine, my dear. Take it from me. And I will personally be sure to spread the word that—" Her lips curved into a smile as Margo's eyes widened. "That you are the best interior designer in town and that everyone should use your services."

Margo smiled. "Thank you, Dottie."

She smiled as she turned to go. Oyster Bay was full of surprises. At every turn.

*

Every Wednesday night and every other Saturday night. That was the deal Bridget and Ryan had agreed to when it came to sharing custody of Emma. Of course, there was the splitting of holidays and the sharing of special events. And the occasional time that they didn't stick to the calendar, like today, when Ryan offered to take Emma bowling to make up for last Saturday night.

"Daddy's here!" Emma cried, pulling back from her perch at the front window to run to the door.

Bridget dragged herself from the kitchen, trying to muster up some false cheer for her daughter's sake. Over the years she tried not to let her differences with Ryan show, but it certainly wasn't always easy.

She turned the locks and opened the door, Emma right at her side. Ryan stood on the stoop in a navy sweater and jeans, his brown hair a little tousled, a day's worth of stubble gracing his jaw. In other words, he looked good.

Bridget's mouth thinned. "Emma's all ready to go," she said tightly.

"Great," Ryan said, stepping into the small foyer. Bridget reached for Emma's backpack, which included healthy snacks like apples and some whole wheat crackers, though she very much doubted this would stop Ryan from loading her up on sugary drinks and ice cream and hot dogs. "Actually, before we go, I was hoping to talk."

No. Not this again.

"Ryan..."

"Five minutes. Please."

Bridget stifled a sigh. There was no avoiding it. He was her co-parent and he wanted to talk. What was it going to be? A lady friend moving in with him? A little lean on cash? An engagement?

Her hand shook as she set the backpack back on the

floor.

"Emma, honey, why don't you run to your room and get some coloring books for the car while I talk to Daddy?" She watched her daughter go until she had no choice but to slide her eyes back to Ryan. He was watching her intently. Time to brace herself for it. "What's up?" She folded her arms across her chest, wishing that this space was a little bigger.

"The restaurant's been doing really well lately." Ryan grinned. "We're even thinking of building a second location. Something different. A fish and chips type of place."

Bridget stared flatly at Ryan. Was this seriously what he had come to talk to her about? His restaurant again? He knew how she felt about that place. If she didn't resent it when they were married, she sure as hell did once they were divorced. It wasn't just a drain on their finances, or a distraction from their family, it was the source of endless arguments and bitter fights, and eventually, the reason that all their dreams—or her dreams at least—had ended.

"That's great for you, Ryan," she managed.

"It is. And…I have you to thank for that."

Bridget's eyes popped. "Excuse me?"

"It's because of you that I have what I have. You helped me follow my dreams. You sacrificed a lot."

Bridget's eyes welled with tears, but she looked down quickly at her socked feet. She wouldn't let him see her cry. Not now. Not after all the heartache he'd caused her. At some point, it had to end.

"I know I ruined our family. I know I wasn't always fair to you."

Oh my God, why was he saying this? Now, after all these years? It was too late. Far too late. "It's ancient history," she said quickly.

"Maybe so. But I owe you, Bridget. I owe you for a lot. And I want you to have this."

He handed her a piece of paper, folded in half, and it took Bridget a moment to realize that it was a check. "What? No." She shook her head, daring to look up at him. "Don't you need this for the second place?"

He shook his head. "Take it. It's time for you to follow your dreams."

Her dreams. She hadn't even dared to dream, not about anything other than a real house for her daughter. A real home. *Her* home.

Bridget let out a shaky breath, and opened the check, barely registering the sum that was scrawled out in Ryan's familiar handwriting.

"Ryan." She clamped a hand to her mouth, no longer caring that the tears were falling and that she couldn't stop them if she tried. "It's too much."

"It's not too much. It's what you earned. I can't ever make it up to you," he said. "But I'd like to think that maybe this will help a little. Even if it is about eight years too late."

Bridget swallowed the lump that had settled in her throat. "Thank you, Ryan."

His eyes crinkled at the corners when he smiled, and for the first time in so long, she saw a glimpse of the boy she'd once fallen in love with, the one with the sweet comments and the nice laugh and the good heart.

"Mommy!" Emma exclaimed as she ran back into the foyer, arms full of princess-themed coloring books. "Why are you crying? Are you sad that I'm going bowling with Daddy and you can't come?"

"Not sad, honey." Bridget smiled. "I'm happy."

"You're welcome to join us," Ryan said, taking Emma's hand.

It was another step, an invitation that was in her hands, and her answer would determine if she would stay rooted in the past, or move forward.

"Please come, Mommy!"

Bridget thought of the laundry that was piling up, the stack of bills she had planned to pay, and the vacuuming that needed to be done. And she thought of the man who had broken her heart and her dreams and left her to struggle as a single mother for eight years while he did everything he pleased. And she looked into the eyes of the man who was standing here now, the father of her child, asking her to put it all behind them.

"I'd like that," she said.

Ryan grinned, and for the first time in longer than she could remember, she smiled back.

Tomorrow she would do the laundry and clean the kitchen and worry about Mimi and find that field trip permission slip. Or maybe…maybe she'd invite her sisters for brunch tomorrow. And for once, she wouldn't allow herself to think of all the practical things she could be doing with her time instead.

Chapter Sixteen

Sunday mornings at Pete's Diner were always crowded, and it took Margo a moment to find her sisters through the crowd. But there they were, at a back table, Abby in a green sweater and Bridget in blue, both looking happier than she'd seen them since she first came back to town.

"There you are!" Abby said, pushing a chair away from the table to allow Margo to join them.

"I see the party's already started," Margo observed. She flipped over her coffee mug and lifted the carafe in the center of the table.

"Oh, just a little girl talk," Abby said. "There's a new cute guy working over at Serenity Hills."

"A male nurse," Bridget informed her.

Margo kept her expression neutral. He already sounded better than Abby's last guy.

"I think I'll pay Mimi an extra visit today," Abby mused, giving them a knowing smile.

"I might join you," Margo said. "If you promise to distract that cat while I'm there."

"As long as you don't try to flirt with Mr. Wonderful." Abby grinned. "But then, you're no threat. It's Bridget who's single."

"And not looking," Bridget added with a stern look.

"Actually…" Margo took a deep breath. "Ash and I are over."

Bridget's brow creased in concern. "You sure about that?"

Margo nodded. She'd never been more sure of anything. "It's over. And…I'm okay with that."

"I'm sorry, Margo." Bridget gave her a sympathetic look. "I know it isn't easy to end a marriage, even when it isn't working."

Abby didn't seem to know how to react. She looked from Margo to Bridget and back again. "So what does this mean? Are you…divorced?"

Divorced. It was such a big word. So official. "Eventually. It's better this way," Margo said, taking a sip of her coffee. "I know it in my heart." And Mom knew it too, she thought. But there were some things in life you had to discover on your own. "Ash and I had some good memories. I'm going to try to focus on that. It wasn't all for nothing."

"I feel the same way about Ryan," Bridget announced,

and now it was Margo's turn to glance at Abby. "Actually, Ryan and I have decided to try to be friends. For Emma's sake. We're going to try to get along better, maybe even do an outing every few months, so Emma can have both of her parents together."

"How do you feel about that?" Margo gauged. Usually the mere mention of Ryan's name was enough to cause Bridget's cheeks to flush and her eyes to narrow.

But now Bridget smiled. A real, genuine smile of contentment. "I feel...relieved. And I feel...relaxed. I'd been holding onto anger for so long that I couldn't even think of what I ever saw in that man to begin with. He's not a bad person. He's just not someone I should be married to."

Margo nodded. She felt the same way about Ash, somehow. Not that she'd be forgiving his recent behavior, though.

"There's more," Bridget said. "It's why I asked you guys to come to brunch today."

Margo's stomach dropped. Oh, God. The house. She'd done it. It was official. The house was sold.

"I'm not selling the house." She looked at them expectantly, as silence fell over the table.

"What?" Abby looked distressed. "But how can you say that? You said we needed the money to pay for Mimi—"

Bridget was shaking her head, but she was smiling. "It's not going to be a problem. I'm buying the house."

"You?" Margo could only stare at her sister. "But

how?"

"You know all that money I gave Ryan for his restaurant?"

Did Margo ever know. She knew every detail of every sacrifice. Every dream that Bridget had, however small, overshadowed by Dunley's. Every dime that Bridget earned back then went to pay for contractors or liquor licenses or a new industrial-sized fridge.

"He paid me back." Bridget was beaming. "All these years later, he made it up to me for helping him build that restaurant into what it's become. And it's enough money to live on for a while, too, especially if I turn the house into a business."

"A business?" Margo noticed the waiter approaching their table from her periphery, but from the way all three women were hunched over, rapt in conversation, he thought better of it and moved on to the next table instead.

"I'm going to turn the house into an inn. With your blessings, of course."

"As if you needed to ask!" Margo exclaimed. "That's a fantastic idea! Do you need any help?"

"Actually, I was hoping you could help me redecorate. Turn the bedrooms into guest rooms, that type of thing. I have some experience from when I worked in the hotel, and I already have a list of ideas I want to incorporate. I was up all night planning things!" She beamed, and Margo realized it had been a long time since she'd seen her sister smile like that. "I'll bring in a contractor for some of the work, like transforming the attic and closing off some of the downstairs space for a small apartment for me and Emma. But…you approve?"

"A hundred percent, yes!" Margo's cheeks hurt from smiling so much, and Abby flagged down the waiter, who looked guardedly at the ruckus they were all causing now.

"Three mimosas," she declared. "We're celebrating today."

The waiter hurried away, but that didn't stop Abby from lifting her coffee mug while they waited. "A toast. To family. And…to bright futures."

"To bright futures!" Margo and Bridget declared.

It was true that perhaps the future had never been brighter, for any of them. There was just one thing missing, though, Margo thought. A person she had always seen in her future, one she had forced herself to forget, and now, couldn't again. Would Eddie ever speak to her again? Or had he made up his mind, was he going back to Philly?

It was Sunday. His decision was made. She frowned when she thought that it might be too late for them. That they'd wasted another opportunity. Or that maybe, they just weren't meant to be.

Bridget caught her frowning. "You okay?"

"I am," Margo said slowly. "And I will be okay."

Abby set down her mug and sighed. "Now that you guys have everything figured out, I guess that just leaves me."

"Are you saying that you're looking to settle down?" Margo glanced at Bridget, who looked just as perplexed as she felt.

Abby laughed. "God no. Life is too short to stay put, doing the same thing day after day, with the same person…"

Margo smiled at Bridget across the table as the waiter appeared with their drinks. Maybe she was wrong. Some things did never change.

*

If there was one advantage to small town life, it was that you could easily find someone. And if you didn't know where they were, you could ask. One question to Bridget confirmed that she'd seen Eddie at the apartment building that morning, and that he usually had Sundays off, too.

And this was why, with a pounding heart, Margo stood in the courtyard of the building, staring at Eddie's door (information also courtesy of Bridget) wondering if he would even answer it when she knocked.

She had to try.

She put her fist to the door and, before her nerves could get the better of her, tapped three times.

Nothing happened. Maybe she hadn't knocked hard enough. She tried again, a little louder this time.

Nothing. She stared at the door, wondering if he was inside and choosing not to answer, or if he was gone and she should come back later. She reached into her handbag for a scrap of paper and scrawled a note that she tucked under the corner of his doormat.

"Looking for me?" a voice behind her said, causing her to jump.

Margo turned, heart pounding, to see Eddie standing a few feet from her, a strange expression on his face that she wouldn't exactly define as a smile.

"I was just leaving you a note," she said. As if that weren't obvious.

"A note?" Now Eddie looked interested. "What does it say?"

Now why'd she have to go and leave a note? Why hadn't she turned and left, come back later? She sighed against her growing humiliation and reached down to grab the paper, which she thrust out at him.

He took it and read aloud, "I'm sorry. Margo." He looked up at her. "Sorry for what?"

Margo froze. This was where her grand plan ended, and it hadn't been much of a plan at all, really. "I'm sorry for the other day. At my house."

Eddie held up a hand. "No need to apologize." But his jaw was set and his eyes were flat and Margo knew then what she was sorry for, and what she'd been afraid to say earlier, for fear that it wasn't really true.

"I'm sorry if I hurt your feelings. I'm sorry if you thought…Look, Ash surprised me. I wasn't expecting him."

Eddie just nodded. "It's your life, Margo. I'm not

involved." He tried to brush past her, toward his door. He was already fetching his key from his pocket.

"But you are involved," she said, her voice growing louder, forcing Eddie to stop walking. "You were...always involved."

Eddie frowned, and Margo felt her shoulders droop. She motioned to the sidewalk. "Can we take a walk? Just five minutes? I feel like everyone's staring out their windows."

He looked up. "I'm sure they are." He hesitated. "I guess I can spare five minutes."

That wasn't the reaction she had hoped for. Still, she'd take it. They walked out of the courtyard and down the street, to a park she used to play in as a child. The park where he'd first kissed her, half a lifetime ago. Leaves crunched under feet, and children laughed in the distance. Margo kept walking, hoping it wasn't too late, that Eddie hadn't made his decision. That he wasn't leaving. Again.

"When you left...it broke my heart," she said. She couldn't look at him, just at the leaves beneath her shoes, and the tufts of grass that wouldn't be green much longer. "And I didn't want to feel that way again. I didn't want to fall so hard. And then I met Ash." She shrugged. "And it was easy." Now she turned to look at him. "I tried to find someone as different from you as I could. It seemed like the only way to guarantee that I'd never feel the way I felt when you left me. But I didn't stop to realize that I never felt the way I did when I was with you either. Happy.

Excited." She shook her head. So many wonderful feelings that couldn't be put into words. "Ash and I are over. I told him so."

"Because of what happened?" Eddie asked, stopping to look at her properly.

"Because of that, yes. But because...we weren't right for each other, not really. And because I gave up so much to try to convince myself that we were."

"And what is right for you, Margo?"

Margo took a deep breath. She didn't want to tell Eddie how she felt. She didn't want to give him that power again. But if she didn't, he might never know.

"You were right for me," she said, swallowing hard. "Maybe...maybe you still are."

Eddie grinned. A slow, smooth grin that made her stomach flutter and her chest swell. "You know when I went over there and saw you with him, I was pretty upset."

She nodded. "I know."

"I got in my car, and I drove around."

She knew where this was going. "And you called Mick."

He raised an eyebrow. "And I called Mick."

Oh, God. Margo chewed her lip. "And what did you decide?"

"Philly was good to me, Margo. It's where I became a cop, it's where I started helping people and really, well, growing up, I guess you could say." He stared at her for a moment. "It's time to put down roots. Time to go home."

She nodded. Of course, of course. It made sense. Why would she have thought he'd want to stay? He didn't have fond memories of this town, not like her. It was never his home, it was only ever a place he'd passed through.

"So I'm staying."

She blinked. "What?" Her heart was pounding and she hadn't even realized she had been holding her breath until it came out in one long burst.

His grin was slow. "Oyster Bay is where I belong. It's where I've always belonged. It's where I've been happiest. I never forgot the time I spent here. The time I spent with you."

She couldn't hide her smile. "Oh."

"And what about you? You thinking of giving Oyster Bay another shot?"

"I am, actually," she said, grinning up at him. "I ran away for all the wrong reasons."

"And now?"

She looked at him, at the man who had stolen her heart, and who still had it. "Now I have a reason to stay."

"Think the second time around will be just as sweet?" he asked, reaching down to take her hand. It was warm and smooth and achingly familiar.

"Even sweeter," she said, knowing it was true. That they'd both come so far, and full circle, to be standing right here in this moment. "But no rush this time. I need some time and—"

"Take all the time you need," he said, leaning in to kiss her. "I'm not going anywhere."

And neither was she.

Coming Soon

ALONG CAME YOU

Single mom Bridget Harper has no time for romance. Her hands are full enough running her new inn. Toss in a sister's wedding to host, another sister's career to help jumpstart, and a grandmother's missing cat to find, and Bridget has little free time for anything other than taking a good book down to the beach. With troubled times officially behind her, she's perfectly content with her busy life...until a handsome guest has her questioning what may be missing.

Novelist Jack Riley came to Oyster Bay with one purpose only: to write. With a deadline looming, he plans to lock himself inside his room at a remote country inn, and not emerge until his work is finished. The trouble is, he came to get away from distraction and, thanks to the irresistible innkeeper, finds it at every turn. Dragging out his stay in this small town is the last thing he had in mind, until he begins to wonder if he's finally found his muse...

OLIVIA MILES writes feel-good women's fiction and heartwarming contemporary romance that is best known for her quirky side characters and charming small town settings. She lives just outside Chicago with her husband, young daughter, and two ridiculously pampered pups.

Olivia loves connecting with readers. Please visit her website at www.OliviaMilesBooks.com to learn more.